D0122295

# THE GREEN HOUR

# THE
# GREEN
# HOUR

*Frederic Tuten*

W. W. NORTON & COMPANY

NEW YORK   LONDON

Frontispiece: Nicolas Poussin. *Echo and Narcissus.* Oil on canvas, 74 x 100 cm.
The Louvre, Paris, France. Photo: Erich Lessing / Art Resource, NY.

For information about permission to reproduce selections from this book,
write to Permissions, W. W. Norton & Company, Inc., 500 Fifth Avenue,
New York, NY 10110

The text of this book is composed in Garamond MT
Composition by Sue Carlson
Manufacturing by Quebecor Fairfield
Book design by Lovedog Studio
Production manager: Julia Druskin

LIBRARY OF CONGRESS CATALOGING-IN-PUBLICATION DATA
Tuten, Frederic.
The green hour : a novel / by Frederic Tuten.
p. cm.
**ISBN 0-393-05105-6**
1. Triangles (Interpersonal relationships)—Fiction. 2. Capitalists and financiers—
Fiction. 3. Woman art historians—Fiction. 4. Radicals—Fiction. I. Title.

PS3570.U78 G74 2002
813'.54—dc21                    2002069215

W. W. Norton & Company, Inc., 500 Fifth Avenue, New York, N.Y. 10110
www.wwnorton.com

W. W. Norton & Company Ltd., Castle House, 75/76 Wells Street,
London W1T 3QT

1 2 3 4 5 6 7 8 9 0

*For Karen Marta*

Serán ceniza,
   mas tendrá sentido,
Polvo serán,
   mas polvo enamorado.

—*Francisco de Quevedo y Villegas*
*(1580–1645)*


Ashes they will become,
   but not their feelings,
Dust they will become,
   but dust in love.

# THE GREEN HOUR

# CHAPTER I

I T WAS AN unlikely bar. At the bottom of an old hotel on the river. Smoky. With a few heavy leather armchairs facing the banquettes and small round tables; low, mellow light that made you sleepy in a pleasant way. It was far from him, at the other end of Paris, but she knew he had chosen it for her, remembering she found it elegant.

"And now? How is it now?" he asked.

She had been ill and now she wasn't. The disease—checked in time, as the doctors were fond of saying—bombarded and sent into hiding for five years, ten years, perhaps forever. Surviving cells hiding, perhaps, in some cave of herself that the chemical bombs did not reach and waiting for the "all clear" signal to emerge and return to their work, to their feast.

"I'm still fine," she answered. "But who knows day by day?" she added, qualifying the certainty of her answer so as not to pique the capricious gods.

He had asked after her health periodically over the past five years, even phoning her from Europe when he was away, so she knew his inquiries were more than politeness.

He was glad, he said. She knew he was, that he really was, but now she wanted to enliven the atmosphere and return it to the occasion, which he had skirted since they met that evening.

"I would have thought you would've asked a few friends to celebrate with you," she said.

"With us," he said. He gave her an affectionate, sly smile and raised his glass in salute.

"But it's *your* birthday, Samuel." It was still strange, even now, years after being colleagues, to hear herself call him anything but Professor Morin, her former thesis adviser, mentor, older friend, and now her protector at the university where they both taught.

He waved his hand, as he had always done when she brought the conversation to him, as if to say, I'm of no importance, let's move on. She didn't press him. There was much else to talk about, in any case. What had he been doing, working on, in the year she had not seen him?

What he was working on was turning seventy, he said, enjoying dividing his time between Paris and New York, teaching every other year. And now he was enjoying drinking at the Pont Royal with her, who still seemed, astonishingly to him, the young woman in her twenties who first stepped into his seminar on Goya. That's what he was working on, enjoying himself.

It was *her* work he was interested in. As always. He still had that solicitous air which had always made her feel protected and young. At forty, she still was his protégée and was still happy to be nestled between the pinstripes of his old-fashioned wide lapels.

"Poussin," she said apologetically. Apologizing as much to

herself as to him, for the years that had passed without a book to show for them. It was to be her second major work since the publication of her doctoral thesis on Goya's cartoons for tapestries, which demonstrated, contrary to current scholarship, that scenes of picnics, kite flying, dance, and children at play were not merely documentary reflections of contemporary life but were rich with metaphor and allegory on human frailty and the transitory nature of life. This was the study that had propelled her career and academic reputation years earlier.

She was summering in Paris to complete the Poussin book, she said, which, of course, was just a pretext to come to be with him, she added, with a smile.

"Would that it were so," he answered.

"And why not?" she asked in the same flirtatious vein. It was Paris and the drinks had made her a little giddy, although she had been feeling like that ever since she woke that morning; the May sun with the morning coffee, the Louvre and Poussin waiting for her in the afternoon, Professor Morin in the evening.

"That business was decided ages ago, when you wrote me that charming postcard from Madrid, when you were still writing your thesis."

"Weren't they all charming?" she asked.

"I'm referring to the one where you said you loved only Goya and Professor Morin."

"Well, it was somewhat true, Samuel," she said, with airy emphasis.

"My only rival, you said, was Goya."

"Well, it's still true. I don't think of Poussin in that way."

"That was delightful, what you wrote, Dominique. But it's

what you say to an older man you've decided never to be with. And of course it reminded me to keep my place. The helpful mentor."

"For which I have always been grateful," she said.

He laughed, a little tightly. "I would have loved such a friend for myself."

She felt two little jabs at once. One for the shame of having disappointed him as a friend, though she had not been aware or been made aware that he had ever felt her friendship lacking. And the other and the more keen, the recalling suddenly that his birthday was also the anniversary of an event they had obliterated from their conversations, and which she had deliberately erased for long stretches of her memory.

She had been his graduate student, his most exciting reason for teaching; he admired the fresh and personal—sometimes too much so—way she wrote about paintings. He was envious of all the wonderful books she had yet to read and write. She had found such declarations in notes stuck between the returned pages of her manuscripts, along with his insightful commentaries on the direction of her work. Beside her contention that Goya's "Black Paintings" "radiated the world's invisible darkness the way radium does its poisonous green rays," he had written: "Stay away from chemistry, it's not your field—neither is poetry." Bracing, that.

"I thought all that was settled long ago, Samuel," she said tenderly. "Why didn't you ever tell me what you were really still feeling?" she asked, realizing the serious matter of love underlying the evening's light conversation and banter.

He began as if to make an explanation but then caught himself, shrugged his shoulders to emphasize his joke.

"I waited to turn seventy," he said. He smiled. His eyes did not.

"I'm sorry, Samuel," she said. "I didn't mean to be so blind."

"We should just let it go," he said, with another wave of his hand.

He was always a wise man, the wisest. Now he seemed just another man flattened by unrequited love. She had woken many mornings to find herself similarly flattened, a longing silhouette in the mirror. She wanted to reach out and touch his face but she was afraid he would take the gesture for charity and not the sign of affinity—of warmth for him—she would have meant it.

By the time she completed her course work, they had already passed beyond the formal boundary between student and teacher and had become friends. Some thought they had become lovers, but they had not. She was already occupied in that department. Sometimes she went to his small apartment crowded with books, journals, and manuscripts stacked haphazardly on the floor, even in the kitchen, and cooked him dinner. Grilled sole, her specialty, with a delicate caper sauce, the way her mother had taught her to prepare it.

They read, smoked cigarettes; she, thinking them *chic*, the strong dark French ones she had heard intellectuals smoked in Paris cafés until she followed the Professor's example and took up Camels; they talked about eighteenth- and nineteenth-century French and Spanish art and on occasion about themselves. More she than he.

She was flattered by his indulgence in letting her express her thoughts, which were so unformed beside his. She felt adult with him, let in on the ways of the urbane intellectual world, where rarefied ideas removed one from the dreariness of ordinary life, removed one from being ordinary, one of her great fears.

In her senior year at college she had thought herself somewhat a Marxist, believing in the universal need to narrow class and economic distinctions, but not caring so much for Marxist doctrine, which she found claustrophobic and, as she told him, aesthetically stale. He appreciated her moral side as he did her aesthetic passions and did not make her feel—what she herself deeply felt—that her thoughts were wanting experience.

She had found him attractive at times, mostly when he had least prepared himself to appear so. When some stubble had gone unshaven on his chin, when his tie and jacket were spotted with egg drippings, even in class. She liked him when he was tired, sitting in his worn armchair, white shirt open at the neck, his eyelids droopy, a cigarette between his yellowing fingers, a book in French or German on his lap. He looked oldish, but not like an old man; he looked like a page torn from Europe before the war, which he was, no matter how long he had lived in America.

She was his America. The best the culture had produced. Serious, but not weighted by the scholasticism and pedantry of her European graduate student counterparts. Of course, like most Americans, she did not know anything, and that accounted for her lightness. She was open to new circuits of thinking and unencumbered by doctrine—as her lackadaisical, unexamined, and eclectic social philosophy had shown—and she was supple.

"My mind?" she asked.

"That, too," he answered with a rare laugh.

He liked the way she was respectful of his learning and

how she did not let that stifle her opinions or their ironic expression. Her tongue sometimes had the bite of film noir dialogue, the language he found essentially and wonderfully American, although no one he knew seemed to speak it in life except she.

"Why don't you let me come over and clean up this dump?" she said one evening, when they were starting to become friends.

He had been offended by her directness and brooded about it for days, he later told her, but he found a housekeeper the following week. "Come over and see the dump," he said. Proudly, she thought.

Everything had been dusted, cleaned, and polished; the windows shone, and the books climbed in formal pillars. He must have brought in a battalion of cleaners to do the job.

"Don't say 'dump,' Samuel," she said, after approving the makeover. "It doesn't suit you."

He did not use the word again, nor did he make any further attempts to be current and colloquial; it did not fit him, he said, as if he had chosen never again to wear a bow tie or a handkerchief in his breast pocket.

He had no wife, never referred to having had one; no girlfriend that she knew of or that he let her know about; she never had seen evidences of a woman's—or man's—presence in the apartment. She did not ask about that part of his life, although she had talked about herself, about Rex—not too often, because she felt him stiffen when she did.

Shortly before she left for a year in Madrid to research her doctoral thesis on Goya, he phoned and asked her to accompany him to the opera the following week. Ordinarily he was indifferent to practical matters, his grades were usually turned in late, the recorded and signed sheets still in his desk drawer where he had forgotten them before leaving on vacation or sabbatical. But he had the wherewithal to arrange for her grant to Spain; had written a long letter of nomination, pushed for her candidacy with the award committee—though he was never known to press for his own advancement within the university—and had shepherded the process through to the signing of the check.

She thought that his invitation was meant to celebrate her grant but he made no mention of it on the phone or when she met him at the Oak Room. He was waiting at a little round table with an unopened bottle of champagne chilling in the bucket; he rose, made a slow bow, and helped her into the chair.

He was absurdly old-world but touching. His gray pin-striped suit was clean and pressed, his tie unspotted. She was sure his shoes were polished and the laces neatly tied.

"It's my birthday," he said softly.

She was happy at first, her mood festive and warm, but by the time they had finished the champagne and were in the cab she felt trapped in sadness. His loneliness moved and repelled her, feeling as if he had invited her to share the burden of his isolation. Where, apart from the university and writing learned books and articles—apart from her—was his life?

She had never sat in the orchestra before, so close up to the stage that she could actually see the singers' faces, eyes, and expressions and not just blotches of heads atop costumes viewed from the clouds. She was disappointed to see that the audience was not well dressed—as she would later describe it—surprisingly so because she always had imagined that orchestra goers wore tuxes and evening dresses, that they were elegant. When she grew up in Montauk, women did not wear gowns, except at a wedding, and the polyester tuxes were rented, up island, in Southampton.

The music was the elegant thing, with an eighteenth-century formal balance and structure, whose prescribed shape was bent by the daring of the artist. Her kind of art. As valued as passion and sometimes more.

It was an opera they both loved, *Così Fan Tutte*; he played it often when she visited, on old-fashioned vinyl disks that revolved at thirty-three and a third revolutions per minute. When they returned from intermission and champagne at the bar she was a little tipsy; he was too, she thought. She liked the feeling of being a bit above the world and of being with him, who seemed so comfortable in that lofty sphere. She brushed his hand on impulse, wanting to say how much she admired him, perhaps even loved him, even his loneliness, which now seemed abstractly noble, like the music as it rose and rose. He drew back as if she had touched him by accident but then he turned to look at her, taking her hand to his lips.

She never told Rex, even years later. Rex had no rights to her in any case, having left her with no declared bond between them. But she would have said that what had happened was the culmination of all she and the Professor had previously shared, their loneliness included. She would have said that she was carried by the wave of wanting to love a man other than Rex.

They left the opera, and Rex was there with them in the taxi when, in a husky voice, Samuel asked, "Will you come home with me?"

They stopped for three red lights before she answered, not that the time waiting was spent in her making a decision; she had made it before Samuel had asked. She thought that only by the Professor's asking her to come with him would the presence seated beside the driver disappear. Which he did until almost the morning.

Rex might not have shown up again or at least not for a long time had the Professor's apartment been less bursting with love. And not just in the bedroom that night, when she spread her thighs and caressed the older man's face tenderly and without passion, but in the little alcove where they had their morning coffee.

He had held back cautiously for three years and not only from professional scruples or even from his knowing that she was already and deeply absorbed in another person but from the fear that he would spoil their ever deepening friendship and ruin his—their—chances for love.

"I might have frightened you away," he said.

He was frightening her now, with his disposition at once confessional and implicitly supplicating, but she was searching for a way to bring the apartment back to its usual temperature before the previous evening's events had cranked up the heat. She was still searching when the words rushed unexpectedly out of her, raw and harsh to her ears.

"I love you, too, Samuel, but not that way."

He came around quickly, even excusing himself for his forwardness—he was wise enough to do that, and to let her know that he would never press her or ever make her feel uncomfortable, and that certainly by the time he would see her again—in Madrid or when she returned—all memory of the evening and its aftermath, unless she wanted otherwise, would be erased, preserving only their friendship. He sounded calm, his voice was even, but he looked like a man who had driven off a cliff.

She suspected Professor Morin continued to be in love with her even a year later when she returned to America and he declared casually over dinner that he had resolved certain matters between them, the passion part, but that he would always love her in an affectionate way, always be her friend. She was relieved, hoped that it was true, but the way his eyes met hers made her think otherwise.

She had been afraid to voice her suspicion for the presumption it would have implied, while guiltily knowing that if she kept the tension between them unbroken he would always watch over and protect her. The selfish side apart, she could not consider her life full without his friendship and touching presence in it.

"It's weak," she said, "but I'm really sorry if I have hurt you, Samuel." It was a weak—and worse, a standard—thing to say, but she said it nonetheless. So she added, "Forgive me, I never meant to be cavalier with your feelings."

He smiled, adjusted his tie. "We have both savored our roles, Dominique. We can still return to them." He ordered another round, very elegantly, *"S'il vous plaît,"* with a tired smile attached to the words.

"Do you ever run into him when you're in Paris?" he asked.

He was putting back his armor, bringing the conversation around to her again.

"Never," she said, not bothering to pretend she did not know whom he meant. There was only one "him," after all. The one she had from time to time talked about over lunches and dinners. "But he's kicking around somewhere," she added blithely.

"I think," he said, somewhat sententiously, she thought, "he's still kicking around in you."

It was growing lively at the bar. Editors from the nearby publishing offices were stepping in after work, manuscripts bulging in briefcases at their feet. Dominique knew some of them and smiled as they passed or nodded hello. They looked tired, in the way of editors who for years have taken manuscripts home at night and on weekends.

She recognized Claude, looking worn among the grayish knot at the bar. He gave her a polite smile and nod, then turned away to his friends. She had gone to bed with him a few times, years earlier. He had claimed to be interested in translating and publishing her book on Goya's tapestry cartoons. They were attracted to each other. They went to Deauville for the weekend like a hundred other weekend lovers escaping Paris and their stale marriages—from his stale marriage, from her limbo. Her limbo, inhabited by a wandering shadow.

They drank champagne, she and Claude, as lovers were supposed to do; they screwed on the bed and on the floor, they walked along gray beach and looked out on gray sea—as had other couples in every middling French movie—while the November mists chilled them and returned them to bed. He actually said *"O là là"* when he came. She almost laughed and wondered whether Rex was crying out the same thing in some bed or wherever he was now trying to save the world.

"Kicking around in me," she said, repeating his phrase. "Who knows, Samuel, it's been so long." She knew. She was lying to save face and not seem the fool she was to love a man absent from her in every way except in her mind.

She tried bringing the conversation to other matters, to recall pleasant events in their history, to repair what—without her knowing—had been frayed for many years yet what had seemed to her a whole cloth, but the temper of the evening no longer allowed it. The air turned cool, the wine musty, the service wayward.

He resisted gently any further attempts she made to open his feelings or to cast him once again as the sage and kindly Professor Morin. Had he ever wholly been that or had wanting to love him and be loved by him dispassionately been a convenient fiction of her desire? By the time the check arrived—which she insisted on paying—she felt guilty and misused at once. As if in the middle of his earlier revelation of feelings he had quietly unzipped his fly and let loose his tired old prick, his balls, like rosy old prunes, flopping to the edge of his chair.

They were off, he to his home in Neuilly, where he had been born, where he had lived—as had his great-grandparents—the life of a Frenchman until the Vichy government decreed him and his family deportable Jews. He had gone to America to wait for his parents to follow; he had left in time, they did not. Nor did his friends and relatives. Smoke, ashes. From a fullness of life, they went to zero, except in his memory.

He had told her his story slowly over the years, how various foundations had carried him from being a lonely studious boy to being an isolated but educated man. He was valiant—the old-fashioned word readily came into her mind—and elegant. They would have had a life of thought and companionship, of comfortable travels to museums and concerts and operas, to exotic places—India even—where they would be enriched and from which they would arrive home glad that they had left and glad that they had returned. What more graciousness would one want from life?

She had admired him, loved him, perhaps, but she did not wish to kiss him on the lips or mix her breath with his or lick

his neck after he had just showered and sat wrapped in a towel
by a window overlooking the sea.

"I'm a fool," he said. "I've ruined the evening and who
knows what else."

"Nothing else," she said. She would allow him spoiling the
evening. But then she regretted her discourtesy in allowing
even that. He was a bit shrunken, tired. He had spotted his tie
with wine. It was his birthday.

"I'll always love you, Samuel," she added. She knew she
would, she was always good for the long run.

They made vague plans to meet over the summer. They
kissed on the cheeks three times, the Parisian way. They
hugged. He offered to drop her off at her flat, noting that he
was still not used to leaving a woman alone in the street, however much it was done in America. She thanked him and kissed
him on the cheek. They hugged again. And now they were at
the taxi stand and now he was in the cab waving goodbye.

Though they had spoken of having dinner together, that
plan had vanished. It wasn't yet eight, still light, and she was
alone. She walked down the Boulevard St. Germain promising
herself not to end up at the Café Flor, the seating grounds of
tourists like herself—though with all those Paris years behind
her, she hated thinking of herself as one. Love for a city being
sufficient grounds for citizenship, even if just honorary.

But the Flor would be safe. Rex would never be there. Or in
any of the predictable and for him bourgeois places she now
frequented.

She took a table in a crush of tables and ordered a Kir, to
keep her bittersweet mood intact, to hear herself say the word
that reminded her of Goya's earthen castle with giant hinges

on the open oaken door, a troubled witch flying out from it to the very blue sky.

A man was speaking to her in French. It was halting but good French, with an American accent. The man was speaking politely, the voice was firm, with body, as they say of wine. With quality, she would have added.

# CHAPTER 2

"PLEASE SPEAK ENGLISH," she said.

He did, noting how excellent her English was. She shrugged and gave him a smile, which was perhaps more than he had expected.

But who knew what he expected? She looked him over: strong, black hair cut short, a hawk's beak, clear skin, the rest of him on the square side, but trim. She decided to be cordial, to give him a chance. She would have wanted the same.

"Do me a favor," she said. "Why don't you make up a name for yourself and I'll do the same, just for the sake of conversation. Will you do that? For conversation's sake?" How much easier for her to talk to a stranger while wearing a mask, even a partial one.

He took to it immediately and naturally, she thought. He told her he was on holiday, having spent five years developing an instrument for detecting oil pockets under the coastal seabed, and now he was on a tour of Western Europe, his first, and his first time out of America.

"And you, Alba?" he asked—the name of her quick invention.

Oh! She? She was the American mistress of a rich French banker, a man who loved the cinema and who was starting to produce films, a remake of *The Razor's Edge*. Had he read that novel by Somerset Maugham—an oldie black-and-white film with Tyrone Power? He was going to update it, her man was. Even in joking she thought it a good idea, corny as it sounded—a film about a young American searching for a spiritual life, for a life original to himself.

Actually, he had read it and he had even seen the film. Had read it when starting college, when he was still a dreamer and not sure of his life's path. It's that kind of book, he said, made for dreamy young people off the path.

She disliked him for his certainty, his judgment of youth's idealism. She didn't like the assertive way he had made his cup clink on the saucer as if to emphasize his observation.

"But you've found your path, Eric, haven't you? And what an ambitious and hardworking path it must be, leading you all the way to Paris and to this café." She impolitely turned and asked a man at the next table for a cigarette.

"I'm in luck," he said, "to have it lead me to this table."

Sometimes just talking to a man who seemed interested in her made her jittery and sharp-edged. But he had taken her irony and her slight and did not waver or bridle. It had the effect of calming her, and was a good start, she thought, though for what she was not sure.

"Thank you, Eric," she said. "That was graceful." She had meant it, but somehow she thought she had sounded patronizing. Perhaps she also had meant it to be.

To flirt. The French say *draguer*, to drag, as if seining for fish; all sorts of swimming things getting caught in the net, if you trawl long enough. Perhaps that is why she had been so arch, counting herself just one among the other swimming things he was trying to net in his evening trawl, although, she assured herself, she did not care where he fished; she was unfishable, not swimming, not even near the water, years from a puddle. Finally, she was just a nervous fish out of water.

They walked along the Seine. Maybe they'd run into Rex on a bench and invite him along for the rest of the stroll. He gently offered his arm. She did not take it.

"You're a nice man," she said. "I'm sorry I was so difficult with you before."

He smiled. "Who are you really, Alba?"

"I'm Dominique," she said.

"And you," she asked, "who are you?"

"I'm still Eric," he said. "Eric Wynan. I'm not good at making up names or things."

She laughed.

"You're the most attractive woman I've seen in Paris," he said abruptly.

She turned to look at him, to give him some thought.

"Or New York, for that matter—or just anywhere," he said.

"It's just clothes," she said. "That's all you see."

The clothes: She had a few nice things she had saved up for on a professor's salary, and those she kept with care and wore sparingly.

"And your grace in them. The clothes are extra."

"So, Eric, what do you want?" she asked, as they crossed to the Ile St. Louis. "With me, I mean."

"If you're free, show me the Paris you know."

"A sort of tour guide?" she laughed. "Is that what you want?"

He didn't answer, his head was down—looking for coins on the pavement?—and she gave him a sweep: moccasins without tassels, khaki pants, not baggy, blue cotton shirt, boxy, a gray poplin jacket. She liked the simplicity of his dress, its American wholesomeness.

She stopped at a door of a wonderful building facing the river. She did not live there.

"I'm here," she said.

"I'll send my car for you tomorrow," he said. Adding quickly, "If I may?"

He had taken his first wrong step. He only needed one to make her happy, to assure her once again that there was no one else, never would be anyone else, just men, interchangeable and lacking.

"It's that I don't drive," he said, sensing her withdrawal.

"And I don't travel in cars." She lied, loving cars, large and roomy ones, speedy and silent. "Especially ones sent by strangers to fetch me."

He stood erect, turned to her fully, no longer an eager pup. There was a graying of disappointment in his face: She had pushed him too hard.

"Well, thanks for the walk, anyway," he said.

She heard the quiet "fuck you" in his voice.

He extended his hand. She shook it. He turned to leave. A liveried chauffeur stood by a black sedan and was opening the door.

"Did the car just fall from the sky?" she asked.

"It materializes whenever I imagine it. As I had you, earlier," he answered.

"Look," she said. "I'm usually not like that."

"Like what?"

She laughed at the clever way he had positioned her to answer. "Bitchy," she said. "You knew what I meant."

He gave her a wide smile, studied her, thought her over. She saw his careful side, the one that had helped him to make money, and it was compelling.

"What about tomorrow, then?" he asked.

They made their plan to meet at the top of the artificial mountain in the Buttes-Chaumont, where the surrealists went walking at night, long ago, before Vichy and the Nazi war took away their innocence. She had told him about that, seeing, as she said it, the artists Breton and Aragon strolling though the park at midnight, under a spell they put upon themselves to see the world freshly.

She returned to her room and went to bed immediately, wanting to sleep away the evening's drama. She slept, then woke in the dark.

She lit the room and took a cigarette and read the newspaper. It was the same world. Torture with electric current in Brazil and Argentina; famine and cultural revolution in China; arrests and plots in the Soviet Union; American bombings in Cambodia. How ancient it all sounded. She checked the date and realized it was a decade-old issue of *Le Monde* some former sublet had left behind on the night table. But the events were as fresh as ever, as new as the dawn in her window. All papers the same paper reporting the same news daily but set in different locales and with different names.

She returned to sleep. She'd luxuriate in bed until after

lunch and forget her pointless rendezvous. The best of what they would have, they already had had. Still, she might show up out of decency. She had no idea of how to reach him to say she would not meet him and she knew she would feel bad about leaving him flat. Rex was far away.

# CHAPTER 3

ERIC WAS THERE waiting for her—not knowing, of course, that she had decided at least twice not to meet him—at the miniature Corinthian temple that capped the park's artificial mountain. They looked out across Paris and at the Sacré-Coeur. The site of the Communards' slaughter—of women and children, too, she said. The church was built after the massacre with money and the jewels of the bourgeoisie, to thank God for the victory against the first Communist government in modern history.

She could not resist being didactic, even when flirting.

"Do you find all that history interesting?" she asked.

He nodded and turned to face her and said mostly nothing. He gave her his hand, she gently declined it. He stayed friendly. But as they were halfway on their return down the path, she reached for his arm to let him know she was with him or was in some manner trying to be with him.

"Am I too pedantic?" she asked, knowing she had been even as she asked.

"A tad on the preachy," he replied, still friendly but with a coat of reserve.

"Yes," she said, "that's a bad habit of mine, from having students pretend to listen no matter how much you go on." He didn't speak but extended his hand again and she took it, his so-so hand and OK grip. There was no current going up her arm, although she could feel a hint of some tingle in her imagination.

During lunch, in the café facing the suspension bridge connecting the park to the towering artificial mountain, he kept his reserve but did the talking. She had three Kirs and a Kir Royale; by three-thirty she felt the blood drain from her. The bridge swayed, shaking some lovers crossing it arm in arm.

"Let's go," she said. "But please don't ever talk to me about money, how you earned it from your own ideas and how you had nothing to start with. Don't do it again. And don't try to impress me with a car ride or with anything you think will impress me."

"Well," he said. "I was just anxious and trying to make a dent in you but I didn't know how. I still don't know how."

"Don't do it because it only makes me want to think of someone else," she said, almost pleadingly.

He looked at her intently, waiting for the rest.

"Someone I'd rather not think about."

He came around the table and kissed her, her arms dangling on their sides, her face lifted toward him as if waiting for the dentist to say "Open."

He was at the Ritz, the Coco Chanel suite with a gold bidet and two fax machines. She wanted to tell him that there had been rumors that during the war, Chanel had collaborated with the enemy, as she herself—Rex would remind her—was doing now.

She stayed with him two nights and then made him move out. She hated the waste of money spent on overrated interiors and expensive neighborhoods. He had found it comfortable at the hotel, and as for the money, he did not care. But he moved out, as she had wished. He preferred her to the Ritz, he said.

The bad thing about him, she thought, was his willingness to spend any amount on the principle that it was worth spending lavishly for what was considered the best; the nice thing was that he was not cheap, that he tipped well but not ostentatiously, that at his core he wanted to live, and that money was the least cost. Time, not cash, he said, is the invaluable item.

She liked him for saying that, herself a waster of time, which she too often treated as an inexhaustible bank account. Even after her illness and the threat to her life, she still thought—with the exception of a few bursts of fear—of time as an endless draft, although before the operation, when Rex came to the hospital with his single white rose, she did say, "Rex, how much time do you think we have to go on as we have?"

It had pained her to see Rex, seated against the window light, his hair on fire, his face very white with fear. Never to see him again was the worst side of dying.

"Don't leave me, Red," he said.

She showed Eric her Paris for ten days; he was appreciative of what she had revealed. A guidebook would have shown him much the same, she noted: There were no secrets to Paris, not even for those who lived there; all the secrets were in the history, so where one saw a church atop a hill, another saw a massacre and site of class struggle.

They sat in the Parc Montsouris one afternoon, reading, the leaves of the trees molting the pages of their books, the late-spring breeze tender and endearing, everything was endearing now that she was there beside him, woke with him, sat across from him at all meals in cafés and restaurants.

"What is the world?" Eric asked. "What is its joy?"

"*Quién sabe?*" she answered, with a little shrug. "You tell me."

Her bare arms moved him, the curve of her breasts under the red sweater made him spin. Their being healthy and sexy and smart and in Paris in the spring and in the park reading and knowing they would eventually go back to the hotel and to their soft white wide bed.

"This is the world," he said, "and its only joy."

She laughed. Yes, he was somehow on track, but she wanted really to read right now and to save considering such questions for another time, after they were dead, maybe, when she could weigh her life in the full amplitude of time. Perhaps that was what death was for, she added, the time for looking back on what one should have enjoyed, the living again through memory. To become dust imbued with memory.

"Dust in love," she said, remembering a line from a Spanish poem.

That was a potent image, she thought, unnerving; powder filled with longing, with the memory of its once human love, or better, powder still loving, atoms of dust whirling in desire, emptied of everything but love. It was unsteadying, that image, gave one shivers, like that of seeing, as she now was seeing over Eric's shoulder and in the near distance, a familiar redheaded man striding smoothly through the park and carrying a Japanese child high on his shoulders.

She was despondent the rest of the day and evening, though at dinner she tried to rally and cheer up and even asked Eric to describe his life from the first moment he felt himself a man alive and alone in this world, when he first felt he was who he was. He was pleased, he said, at her interest, considering how she had once asked him never to bring his life to her door.

He described his childhood in the Bronx fondly; no money, a small apartment, where he slept in the living room and did his homework on the kitchen table, not very much food but no hunger, and wonderful books loaned from the public library, where his immigrant parents—German socialists in the tradition of Bebel—loving books themselves, had brought him since childhood.

She, who had lived on the cliffs facing the sea, and on the sea itself working on her father's boat, was suffocated by Eric's small apartment, which she pictured as gloomy and lit by a single bulb in the hall. But she envied him the wonderful books and the parents who had guided his reading—the guiding, not the parents. She could not have wished for better ones than she had.

He had gone to the free City College of New York and later to graduate school on scholarships. Had started in the humanities, in literature, but thought, Why stay poor all my life; I don't have to study books to enjoy reading them, and switched to engineering, the electronic kind. There was something too material about building bridges and buildings, something too fat about it.

She liked his inexplicable "fat," it lent a personal and even poetical quality to his story. She gave him a smile.

"OK," she said. "When are we going to get to the interesting parts?"

He laughed. "The money or the women?"

"A little of both, please," she said.

He did not mean to be boastful, but women liked him— especially when he made his first big money. And even more interesting women appeared from the thin air after he parlayed his invention into a mini-empire, now still growing. There was a soap opera actress on her way to becoming famous in the movies, who never did, and an editor stuck at a fashion magazine who wanted him to marry her and carry her away from a life condemned to the magazine's harem of driven women. He had liked her; he liked the actress, but they lacked a certain emotional autonomy.

Perhaps they had lacked indifference to him, she wanted to say, but she wasn't sure enough to know whether or not it was true or if it was perhaps herself she was thinking about.

He changed the subject, sensing that she really did not want to hear about other women in his life. She did not, feeling that it cheapened him, made him just another man, a rich one with his inventory of conquests, to which one day she would be counted another item.

But even more, her vanity, her snobbism, she admitted, disliked being in the lists with a failed actress of soaps and a desperate fashion editor. She had worked too hard at being independent and free from the popular culture and its shifting values to one day find herself lumped along and devalued with it.

He turned smoothly to the subject of money, about the

beauty of making it beyond the stage of attaining comfort or wealth or even luxury and of reaching a place of abstraction where capital was like a great reservoir of wild electrical charges, of the invisible currents that moved and ran through the world. His aim was to convert those anarchic charges—the dollars that represented them—into movement and power, not just for personal gain but for the way that that power generated human activity everywhere on the globe. For that reason he wanted to expand his interests to include the amassing and enlarging of capital and its transformation into ships, planes, dams, buildings designed by great architects, newspapers that told the truth. He stopped himself, as if to check her reaction.

"Am I being too grandiose?" he asked. "Or too something?"

"Too modest?" She laughed in a friendly way.

She wanted him to know she was trying to be friendly to his ambition, to him. He was packaging himself as the altruistic capitalist, softening the self-serving part. But knowingly or not he was finding the path on which she could join him, if perhaps only partway, herself having once believed that all capital was derived from theft, all capitalist good deeds a mask for rape. How did one live graciously and above the tragic sphere of the ordinary and still not take from the always weaker others?

In her heart she could imagine a life elevated by money. Not comfortable, not sizable, but rarefied amounts that lifted you like a balloon above the earth, where human sadness and its blighted landscape vanished, leaving visible from that height and silence only the world's ravishing contours, shapes, colors, and forms.

She urged him to continue his story and was intent on it, moved, even, from time to time, though even at those moments she sometimes drifted away, her mind drawn to some other scene.

For all his accomplishments, he concluded, for all the happiness his work had brought him, and with all the prospects ahead, he had remained lonely, his life, whoever he was with, shutting down at bedtime.

"Are you lonely now?" she asked, away in some dreamy place of her own loneliness.

"Never with you," he said decisively, and without a hint of sentiment.

It made her feel safe, his businesslike certainty. When the world collapsed and they were the only two left standing and if she asked again whether he was lonely, would he still answer: "Never with you"?

She was certain he would. But even if all the bridges had fallen from the sky and all the buildings had crashed down to earth and they stood alone in the violet light of the world's rubble, she knew she would never answer him the same way.

# CHAPTER 4

OMINIQUE WAS IN her senior year in college and
Rex a year behind, though he, at twenty-one, was her
elder. He had taken a leave from college and had returned a
year later with travel and the sexy aura of mysterious experience behind him. Even though he did not excel at school, as
she did, he seemed exceptional and bound for an unusual life,
with something maverick and glamorous to it.

She thought so even before meeting him, just seeing him
walking alone on campus, drinking coffee alone in the corner
of a local café, or sitting alone, books stacked before him on
the table, in the library. She thought that he had looked up and
glanced at her from time to time, but was not sure. He always
left the library just a few minutes before she did, at midnight,
and she was certain that he went to his room and continued to
read, as she herself did.

She told her friend Rose, the only other young woman on
campus it seemed who did not have a boyfriend or boyfriends
and who was as bookish as she, that she had seen a boy she
thought interesting.

"You mean sexy," Rose said. She was always one to cut to the chase, and for that reason, she said, she was more drawn to the sciences than to the humanities.

"Well, that too. But he's different, I mean."

"No such thing," Rose said. "They are all the same."

She had gone steady once with a boy in high school and well into her sophomore year and she spoke with an authority Dominique did not have.

"Tall with thick red hair. He walks with his head down and is always alone," Dominique said.

"He works in the bookstore. Everyone knows him," Rose said.

"Oh!" The world was closing in and returning to its ordinary scale, the one where everyone knew him.

"He's got tons of girls. I personally know two who have crushes on him."

She wanted to ask whether Rose was one of them, but she did not have to ask.

"Not me, though. He's too skinny and he's too weird."

"Thanks," Dominique said.

"He's different, I mean," she said apologetically.

"Which is what I said to begin with," Dominique said, feeling better.

She had known boys, had slept with one, Glen, when she was nineteen, the year before, in a motel on Montauk Highway. She had been drinking, was her excuse to herself afterward, in her disappointment with the dispassionate sex and its flat romantic wake.

Glen was a physics student. When they first dated she was fascinated with his descriptions of the universe and its roaming mysterious particles, smaller than atoms, than electrons and neutrons. What was ordinary poetry compared to the wildness of ineffable matter?

She had conflated the boy, and his talk of mysterious quarks and neutrinos, with all that was romantically infinite and grand and unknowable. But after the night in the motel, and after some weeks together when they returned to school, and when the need to describe the universe to her was no longer urgent for him, nothing he did or said could any longer compel her, and she was on her own again.

"Hi, Red," he said.

A week after her talk with Rose she went to his café—as she now thought of it—half hoping he would show up. To look at him, even briefly, and measure her idea of him against him. He had come down a bit in height after Rose's saying he had many girlfriends; it was his aloneness and his seeming aloofness from everything but books that had taken her imagination.

"Hi, Red," he said, sitting down at her table.

He went to her directly from the first. She did not think of saying that she thought him rude or aggressive or presumptuous—sitting down as he had, uninvited, calling her Red, as if reducing her to a color—she had not thought him any of those things. She thought: He couldn't be more beautiful.

He offered her a cigarette from his pack of Lucky Strikes. They smoked. She decided not to speak and see how long he could bear it before he made some accommodation to her silence or before he left. All those women with crushes on him, all the tons of girlfriends; she'd wait him out—instinct told her to do so.

She finished the cigarette, crushed it out in the saucer. His eyes were green. She finished her coffee. She paid and rose. He walked out with her and walked beside her in the street. His nose broke to the left. Side by side, they climbed the library steps and stopped at the entrance door. It was fall and some darkish leaves scrapped about their feet.

"I'm getting off here, Red," he said, with a slow smile.

She looked at him fully, knowing after meeting him at the café and walking with him in the street that this exact moment would arrive and knowing what she would say when it did.

"Don't," she said.

# CHAPTER 5

T HEY STAYED IN bed long afternoons after class and read and made love and talked and drank cold tequila in rows of shot glasses. A haze of blue, sexy smoke from cigarettes in ashtrays curtained the room and filtered the light from the window.

"Mexico," he answered. More than a year there. He could have stayed all his life, he might one day do so.

"Not without me," she said.

"Never without you."

It had a soul, Mexico, and a great revolutionary tradition. One day they'd finish off what Zapata and the other great radicals had started and make a true socialist revolution with a socialist society, with freedom and creativity, not like the police state the Russians had created. All the artists he had met in Mexico were for the revolution, and the writers, and the students, and all his friends—and they weren't just playing at revolution, like the rich kids with guilty consciences in North America.

"And you?" she asked.

Neither rich nor guilty. He was a scholarship student like her, and like her came from working-class parents. He'd allow her parents that even though her father owned a small fishing boat, he was hardly a capitalist, an owner of the means of production.

"I'm glad the Commissar will allow them that," she said, poking his ribs.

"The Mexican students alone could bring the whole society down," he said, letting her remark pass. "The French students almost did it in Paris in '68."

"Well, where have they been in the past three years?" she asked.

In any case, the mechanics of revolution did not interest her, she told him, his lips did. He rolled over to her and bit her inner thighs; she parted them.

They slept and woke and made strong coffee and returned to a bed piled with books. For the moment, he was reading Marcuse's *Eros and Civilization*, but he was also reading twelve other books; she watched him going from one to another, some buried under his pillow, some tottering on the night table. Keen on Castaneda's *The Teachings of Don Juan*, he asked her whether she thought one could be a materialist and a mystic at the same time, believing, he said, the world was vast and mysterious enough to allow for both.

"Why not?" she said, if the world didn't allow it she would.

He was officially studying philosophy—she admired the dreamy impracticality of it, while wondering what was ever to become of him, considering he vowed that, unlike her, he would never teach—but he was reading less philosophy and more poetry, Auden his champion.

She loved seeing Rex disappear into his books, knowing he

would return to her and look at her with the eyes of a man
long gone at sea. She loved his return.

"No talking," he'd say. "Come on over here, Red, and let's
see what's doing."

Before meeting him, she had been the campus bookworm
and isolate, now there were two of the same breed, isolated
together. Yet even from bed she kept an eye on the world,
going to classes and taking exams and writing papers. By
spring, she had been accepted into a prestigious New York
graduate school on full scholarship with a money stipend.

Rare, and especially rare for someone as young as she. Her
undergraduate thesis on Goya's "Black Paintings," sent in with
her application, had caught the eye of a noted scholar of
Spanish painting, she later learned; an art historian whose writ-
ings she admired and whose work she had cited often in her
essays and footnotes. She was on her way, Rex said. He was
glad for her.

She worried about him throughout the year. He cut classes
often and had taken some incompletes. He would read three
or four times the amount required for a class but was unable
to complete the term paper, writing draft after draft, footnotes
sometimes half a page long. His test essays were more concerned with the peripheral—more germane to him—than the
central material of the question asked. For a question on the
influence of Rimbaud on the French Symbolist poets he wrote
four blue books on the fall of the Paris Commune of 1870 and
the consequent withdrawal of poets into an ivory tower of
personal and esoteric imagery. At the rate he was going, she
feared he would lose his scholarship for the following year.

"It's all right, Red," he said. "I'll work it out."

It broke her heart to see him going about in circles of his

own making. She suggested they see each other less, at least for the while he should be focusing on getting his work done. Days later, they would be back to their old schedule of reading, sleeping, and lovemaking.

"It's worse if I stay away," he said. So he didn't.

When she returned home for the summer to work as usual on her father's fishing boat, she took him with her. In deference to her parents' feelings, she found him a room in town, living with him on days off and cooking for him and washing out his clothes. The little bourgeois housewife, Rex called her. She had not yet learned, she answered, to separate her affection for a man from old-style domesticity.

"I like him," her father said, unasked, after a week at sea together. Her mother liked him, too, but with a friendly wariness. Rex did not press himself on them, or make winning gestures. He maintained a cordial deference and kept a correct distance from their daughter. In his favor, also, was that although he was generally loquacious when alone with her, in their presence he spoke as little as they did and was as reserved as they were.

He took to the sea, learning the names and positions of the stars, pointing them out to her at night as they lay on the wide Montauk cliffs. There the Big and Little Dipper, there Orion's Belt—the sky deepening to the end of the world. She could set course by them at fifteen, when she took the night watch on her father's trawler while he and the mate, Mike, napped in the cribbed quarters below. She alone on a deck of sea swells, in the heave and pitch of sea in a night of pounding stars. Frightening that was, feeling herself overwhelmed yet exhilarated by the space and the heaving dark water.

Mystery and disquietude—what she eventually found in art

at its deepest pitch. Standing apart and yet belonging to the world, like the pictures she pored over as a child of nine in *A Treasury of Great Paintings*, one of the few books, along with the Bible and *The Settlement Cook Book*, belonging to the house. Her favorite painting, *The Arcadian Shepherds*, by Poussin, was the most mysterious and unworldly in the book, even more than Goya's frightening painting of a giant, as tall as the clouds, eating his son, head first.

Poussin had painted three young and beautiful shepherds and a serene woman by a stone tomb, all under an open sky clouding in the distance. Some thin trees of the kind she never before had seen hovered over tomb and shepherds. One of whom was kneeling reading an inscription, "*et in Arcadia ego*," carved on the plinth; another was relaying the reader's words to the woman, who looked as if she had already heard them, looking as if she understood everything in the world.

Her grade school teacher had told her the meaning of the inscribed words: "Even in Arcadia I am," they said. So far away, Arcadia, where the light through the trees, and the trees themselves and the woman and shepherds, and even the tomb itself were bathed in death. For it was Death who had written those words, her teacher said.

It gave her a shiver, that painting, so beautifully unknowable. In spite of all that her teacher had told her, nothing explained the shiver it gave her. Like that she felt just lying beside Rex on the Montauk cliffs or watching him spoon sugar into his coffee, while he read like a man in a trance.

Always reading. Sometimes he would cut short in the middle of speaking to her to pick up a book he was working on, as he would say, and drown himself in the pages for a quarter of an hour before resuming the conversation. She read, but kept some part of herself open to the world; he left the world and himself behind, a snake entranced by the coiling hum of words.

He picked up his head from his book, as if just then remembering she was there. "I love your voice," he said.

She laughed, loving his voice, so far away at times, coming to her from China on a silken string. Even on her father's boat, the slam of the sea did not mute his voice, however much it drowned the sense of his words.

"Delicately put," she said, "but I get the drift." She got all his drifts and currents and pull of undertow.

She was haunted by him, even years later, while walking to teach her class, entering the door to find her students at the seminar table, waiting for her to be wise, to reward them for their wonderful youth, their brilliance; herself—they were sure—knowing nothing—she was sure—of love's dramas and screams which were born in the deepest tissue of the self and bore no relation to the voice of ordinary pleasure.

She'd be speaking normally, casually—authority coming from suggestion rather than assertion—Professor Morin had taught her that—when in midsentence he would appear to her.

"Now, Red, come on over here and let's see what's doing."

When he said to her "You are the sea," as he had said even before he had gone down to sea with her, he did not mean her cunt and its saline wetness, did not mean the ocean as the original womb of all life, as she was sure her cunt was to his life. She was the wet material that had fallen from the archaic sky in an explosion of atoms crashing and merging in the silent blackness.

One day at sea, they dropped anchor, letting the boat drift sluggishly. The nets were fanned out and straining the water, the boat lolling for position. Rex came to her, smiling.

"I'm going up," he said.

Giving her a little wave, he climbed the rig as if born to it. The last cleat lay twenty feet below the mast's top, and the rest of the naked stretch he mounted by wrapping his legs about the smooth pole and inching himself up until, with a smile in her direction, he reached the swaying tip.

She looked up at him; her father and Mike followed her gaze and then turned to her.

"Rex," she called out. "That's not a good idea."

A strange word, "idea," she thought, after hearing herself, when it was an action she was describing.

Many times over the years, she reflected on having used that word that day, when the mast and its rider were tipping to the sea, until, one afternoon, sitting in the Palais Royal garden, reading from Queneau's *Le Chiendent*—the passage where the character of two dimensions discovers the world of ideas and, in that moment of recognition, swells, as a dry sponge just watered, to human fullness—she came to recognize what that word had always meant to her. The idea was the act. Actions were ideas enacted but, for her, the idea itself was its fullness and existed sufficiently without need of the act to complete it.

As when love, when first born, takes hold and gives body to all activity rushing from it, the conception lasting longer than its temporal manifestations, the conception enduring while the body falls away in repetition, in boredom, in aging, in the draining away of everything corporeal.

He took one long dive into the sea, while she and her father and Mike watched his fall. After several moments, when he did not resurface, Mike dove in. She was still shocked at seeing Rex plummet, for some moments not understanding what she had seen: He was up there saluting her and then, without a word, he was cleanly into the sea.

Her father was already reversing the engine when she dove over, just taking off her boots and trousers. She went down ten feet before spinning slowly about but there was nothing of him there and again at another five feet and another five before she was forced to surface for air. He was gone and Mike too, and if she remained longer, freezing and losing focus, she would join them in the darkness. As she began to surface, seemingly from nowhere, a form was floating up toward her, a humped shape passing her as she went up, she gliding up to the air along with it.

It took some while to revive him, but they did, the oxygen mask finally bringing him around and sending blood to his bluing face.

They brought him below deck and removed his clothes and covered him in rough blankets, she thinking how odd it was to see him undressed by men, by her father; to see him clay-white and limp, his head and pubic hair in briny flames. Naked and beautiful he was, and now being touched by others who did not love him and who did not know how even his inert body excited her more than books, than art, than anything human-made.

She had been frightened that he had died and that she would never see him again, not even his drowned corpse, sunk to the blackest deep where no bones, skin, flesh, no fraction of him would keep, not a snip of his hair, not a pinch of his wet dust for her to hold between her fingers; everything of him vanished but memory, which one day, along with her, would vanish too.

But he slowly revived, dazed and heavy as if waking from a deathly sleep in the snow. Indeed, he had been there in the deep, sleeping, and going toward the farthest sleep in relentless, lazy ease, knowing, he said, that he was unable to wake while wanting to wake, and wanting to see her again. In this ever deepening sleep of dreamy cartoon images of fish and eels waiting on line to feed on him, he kept hearing the refrain from an old song, "I only have eyes for you, dear," and thinking, he said, how odd it was, a sentimental song from his father's time coming now to keep him going seconds longer from bursting his lungs and leaving her forever.

"That's what I kept hearing, with an oldie-time orchestra in the background, Tommy Dorsey maybe, and this woman's soft voice singing," he said, drinking coffee with her in the narrow berth of her father's boat. He smiled at her.

"Did you fall or did you jump?" she asked finally, now that the fear had left her and anger had begun to take its place.

"I don't know, Dominique. I was up there looking and looking down at the sea and riding the swells and feeling like a separate piece of the world."

"How will I ever know who you are?" she asked flatly.

"What's there to know?" he said, closing his eyes. "It's all set between us, always was and always will be."

He turned to sleep and she went above deck, her father silent and Mike looking sheepish, naked and chilled in his blanket. They made for port before their usual hour, arriving home in the dark. She silently brought him to his room, where she put him to bed, covered him, and left. He waved her good night as she turned to shut the door.

"Come again soon, you hear?" he said in a mock drawl.

She had no words for him, there were no words for him. He was the hard puzzle she was ashamed of having tried so hard to solve.

"He is what he is," her father said, without a reproach for Rex or for the trouble she felt he had brought them.

Something in her father's looking at the horizon line all his life must have given him that equanimity, she thought years later, the ability to let be what was, which, to her regret, she had never acquired.

He had jumped in, Rex later told her one Sunday afternoon, to defeat reason.

"There's so much of the settled, comfortable life we've been living, Red. I didn't know how tired I was of it until I got to the tip of the mast and felt the true world heaving underneath me."

"Were you tired of me, too?" she asked. "Tired of us?"

"Not you, darling. But all the whole cozy family stuff. We might as well get married and stay at home the rest of our lives. You know, Red, we can drown here on land."

"I don't believe that's why you jumped," she said.

"Maybe you're right, Red."

She was always judging him, he said, however silently. There was nothing to judge, she answered, since his behavior belonged to nothing she deemed rational. That was his point, he said. A pointless one, she answered. He did not come aboard on the second week, and on the third, when fall was in the breeze, he was gone.

To a small upstate New York hotel to be a waiter, to be alone, to think, to read alone, and to feel himself a separate person, to feel himself without the mitigating and vitiating factor of another's presence in his soul.

A letter, crammed with lines marching to the edge of the page and ready to fall off into space, arrived weeks later:

"I never cared much for Keats. Too abstract and too lofty and too full of grand thoughts. But one or two lines of his have touched me, so much so that I believe I acted one out: 'Hyperion arose, and on the stars/Lifted his curvèd lids, and kept them wide/Until it ceased; and still he kept them wide; . . . Forward he stooped over the airy shore,/And plunged all noiseless into the deep night.'

"Do you think poetry changes anything, anyone? Auden says no. I know it does. But he's just protecting the sanctity of his craft, lest he admit that poetry may change us for the worse as well as for the better."

He was not returning to school—he could read philosophy anywhere and poetry too, for that matter. He wanted to work and save up some money and then travel a bit—maybe back to Mexico, where he had a world of passionate friends not hung up on bourgeois achievement. He did not want a replica of a life, he wanted to live originally. She was part of his life, perhaps its deepest, especially if they could cut away from all that was predictable and safe and boring. He loved her, always would, always. No separation could change that, ever.

He was a cliché, she wrote him, too good to finish anything so ordinary as college. In reply, he sent her, without a word of text except his signature, a postcard of the small hotel where he waited tables and was learning, he said in a previous note, how hard ordinary people worked and how brave they were.

He was absurd. Worse, he was unoriginal—the intellectual leaving behind his intellect for the romance of experience. But what did it matter how absurd he was? She loved him, loved how he held his cigarette between his fingers, how he had smelled in bed, how he turned to her at five in the morning in that same bed and said, "Let's see what's doing, Red."

He was gone and she missed him. She was suffering a deep absence, she wrote her friend, Rose, but there was the consolation that Rex was never entirely absent, because there was no one in the world but Rex who was at once alive and also a ghost.

Her father missed him. Her mother remained silent on the subject, as she was on most subjects—to Dominique's relief. At summer's end, she went alone to feel his presence on the Montauk cliffs and to wait for him to sail into sight, from far away, beyond the horizon line, where desperate hopes are born.

# CHAPTER 6

I T WAS LATE spring and she was weeks from finishing
her first year of graduate studies when she saw a sail in the
shape of a postcard. "Dominique, I miss you. Come visit me."
Beneath his signature, he wrote, "I'm working every day."

She was pleased that he had made the effort to pursue her.
But he had put the action in her court, while it should have
been his part to prove his words by taking a bus or hitching a
ride—as he often had—to see her.

She immersed herself in her books, thinking to keep her
mind off him. Let Rex come to her; she had her studies to
look after. But some days after receiving his postcard, she considered the idea that perhaps he was unable to leave work, that
as a hotel waiter—she knew he had done similar work
before—he served tables seven days a week and had one Sunday off a month. He had made his life difficult. She was sad
for him, for his hard work, for his loneliness.

Half on impulse, one weekend she took a bus and went
upstate, thinking to please him with her spontaneity. Through
the screen door of his cabin, she saw him sprawled on his cot,

a young woman sitting naked, except for her black panties, in a chair facing him, her arms hoisted over her head, her eyes shut. He was clothed, a book resting on his lap. She watched them in their silence, jealous of their erotic tableau, hearing only the heavy flies twisting in the warm spring air.

Rex finally spied her and, showing no surprise, rose from the cot and walked to the screen door to greet her.

"Come on in, Dominique," he said, as if he had been expecting her. She turned to leave, but Rex stopped her.

"Don't be silly," he said. "We're just friends. This is Olga, here."

She was not very beautiful, but more beautiful than she. Snake-hipped, her breasts full, her voice husky—everything she knew Rex loved.

"Oh! You're the one he talks about," Olga said.

Rex smiled. "She just made that up. I never talk about you with anyone."

"I'll be leaving now," Dominique said.

"What a good idea," said Olga.

Rex went back to his cot, stretched himself out, his arm under his head.

"Let's not fuss about this, let's not turn this into a bouzh-wah drama," he said.

"Well, what do you think to call it, Rex?" she asked, trying to hide the injury in her voice.

"I think," Olga said, laughing, "that mosts of all he would like the three of us on the bed. I can see it in his eyes."

"In my ice?" Rex said, imitating her pronunciation.

*"En los ojos, hombre!"* Olga said, laughing. "Don't think your Spanish is so wonderful to make funs of me."

"Does he really talk about me?" Dominique asked.

"No, never," Olga replied, dressing herself, jeans first, leaving her breasts naked to the mild spring air. "Except to say that he was with you."

Dominique sat herself at the edge of Rex's cot.

"But he himself keeps you very particular. Very mysterious, he makes you," Olga continued, "the thing of mystery itself."

Dominique laughed in spite of herself. He had made her very mysterious so he could appear more mysterious for being with her.

"So, for you, being with another woman's man is OK?" Dominique asked.

"Who owns persons? Do you owns them?"

"Ladies," Rex said in mock formality, "just relax, we'll all go for a drink in town."

"Another good idea," Olga said. "Maybes you come, too, Dominique."

"Your English is much better than my Spanish will ever be," Dominique said. "So I'll tell you in plain English: If you want him, take him. He's a disaster in bed, if you haven't already noticed."

"With you, maybes he is bad, but with me he is number one, he is the grand champion," Olga said.

"Now, don't go along lying, there, Olga. The truth is, Dominique, I've never touched her, she's just good for looking at and stirring up trouble."

"What a coward you are, a real *cobarde*," Olga said. "Well, then, Dominique, the truth is we should both leaves him. But maybes you should leaves him first."

Olga had a point there. It was time to fish or cut bait—as her father would have said—and go her way. But she found comfort in Rex's claim of simple friendship with Olga, whom he'd known in Mexico. Her father, still in his teens, had fought in the Spanish Civil War with the Republicans and been one of the lucky ones to escape—after Franco and the fascists had won—over the border to France and from there to Mexico.

They were close, from the day they met, he and Olga, without phony inhibitions, as he was close with many of his Mexican friends. That intimacy was one of the reasons he wanted one day to live in Mexico, that, and for the revolution he was sure one day would explode there before anywhere else in the Americas.

She stayed with Rex that night, after the three had downed a bottle of tequila and several cold beers in a local bar and then another half bottle of tequila to excite the night, and to celebrate the theme of Mexico. For all Rex's convincing words, she felt Olga's ghost turn with them in the sheets while Olga herself slept in a motel Rex found for her down the road.

"Now, darling, this is serious," he said, his hand covering his eyes, to deepen his concentration, his voice coming deeply from his masked face.

"I'm going to Mexico for a long while," he said. "You'll come down later when I have the living arrangements sorted out. Olga and all my friends down there will help get us started."

What was he thinking? That she would leave graduate school to join him? If she loved him, he said, she would come down and they would make a clean start, without the tyranny of schools and families, without the corrosive bourgeois notion of achievement. She had no idea of how sweet Mexico was, how beautiful was the language, how free they would be to see the revolution and themselves unfold.

He had no notion of who she was, she said. None. She had

worked hard all her life to create herself, to come out of the slippery guts of her father's fishing boat, out of the coldness of Montauk's black winters, where she was meant to spend her life married to a man who had his own boat or maybe, if she was lucky, to the local high school English teacher. She had gone to college and graduate school because—in case he had not realized—her studies elevated her, as did the paintings she loved. Didn't a life of ideas mean anything to him any longer?

"Don't you want more from your life, Rex, than waiting tables so you can go and hang out in Mexico or wherever?" she said. She was more angry with him for his wanting her to leave school than she was for having found Olga naked in his chair.

He was silent.

"How long can we go on back and forth like this?" she asked finally.

"Forever," he said. "Everything else we do is just a tangent."

She liked him for his certainty; it partly made up for his exodus. She visited him through the summer, dreaming, when she was apart, of when they would meet again and make love.

That fall she returned to graduate school and he went to Mexico City, where, from what she gathered from his letters, he was drifting. He joined many political discussions with artists and students from the university on how to achieve socialism under the shadow of American imperialism; he read *Das Kapital*—again—and found it like an abandoned old factory, whose rusting machinery, even if tooled back to life, could never compete in the modern world. All the same, he said, capitalism was as rotten—but more clever and global in its reach—as it had been in Marx's time.

He wrote some poetry but claimed it was too much like

Pablo Neruda to show her. Still, he sent her a fragment: "Red, like no earth in the Sierras, your hair paints my chest and hides the falling sky." Whatever the influence, she liked that it was something he had drawn from within himself that was just for her, but he did not send her more poems, even after she asked him to.

Rex was living in a small apartment with a young Frenchman, Jean Pierre, who was studying Mexican mural painting. His father wrote a culture page for the Communist paper, *l'Humanité*, in Paris, and every Left Wing door opened for them. What the doors led to he did not say. Parties, she suspected, when he added that Olga sent her regards.

One day in early winter he joined a large demonstration that had gathered at the Zócalo to protest rising tuition at the national university. Riots broke out; some students were shot and Rex was arrested with hundreds of others and beaten in the cells with hundreds of others, the police fond of him particularly, the red gringo, beating him with clubs on his head and shoulders before hosing him down and beating him again.

Deported, he slipped back, returned to Mexico City and then into the countryside, where friends sheltered him. He withdrew into a period of inactivity and reflection—as he called it in a letter:

"I used to believe your returning to school was silly and against us and what I thought was our idea of life, free of institutions and the like. But these days, I'm not too sure of my idea of life. A demonstration is not a revolution, which, should it ever happen here, I suspect, would be soon crushed by the United States. I'm on the faithless side of the dialectic, maybe to come back more radical on the return swing. Fancy, huh?

"I'm glad you did not come down. What would be here for you, except me? I'm still with you, Red."

"You're without substance," she told him, the spring night he showed up unexpectedly on the steps of her brownstone on Tompkins Square Park. His brown overcoat, frayed at the cuffs and hem, hung down to his rubber-soled huaraches; a doll made of corn silk and beaded red eyes stuck through his coat pocket, a pint of Cuervo tequila stuck out from the other.

He gave her a wide smile. *"Hola,"* he said.

There had been no point in writing her in the past few months because he knew he'd arrive before his letters—what with the Mexican mails and the FBI checking every other scrap of paper that came out of Mexico—and he'd tell her in person what no letter could fully say.

And he thought, too, that she'd enjoy the surprise of seeing him. He had been hitching rides for nine days starting from Brownsville, and he smelled of the road, of tar and sun; his hair and chest of Delicados, the sweetish Mexican cigarettes which he smoked one after the other in the darkness of their bed.

"You have no substance," she said to him, after making love.

"God!" he said, his eyes closed, ignoring her or, in fact, unaware of what she had said, so in repose and so in the drowse of her, a solitary red pubic hair fastened to his lip.

"There's nothing like you that ever tasted so good inside and out." He laughed.

She nudged his ribs. "No substance. A hollow man."

He laughed. She too, though she had tried to hold it back. She had only half meant it, still angry with him for the surprise visit, for his leaving her to begin with, and most of all for not having sent him packing the moment she spied him waiting on the steps.

Instead she had said, "So there you are! I was wondering when you'd turn up again."

She said that coolly, at least, keeping back the angry and the loving things she was burning to say when her heart tumbled on seeing him.

And then, in a jolt, they went from the outer to the inner steps, through the doorway to the kitchen, where they drank glasses of water from the tap while scanning each other—and then to the bedroom where they pulled off clothes, buttons ripping away.

He was coming to stay with her, to live together awhile, or maybe finally, as they were obviously and ineluctably meant to do, forever, though perhaps not for the moment forever. He was thinner than usual. Her anger with him and herself trailed behind her pity for him. He had been imprisoned and beaten and kept hungry, alone. His ribs were sticking out, the ribs she had just banged with her elbow. She looked to see if she had left a bruise and bent over and kissed his side.

"I'm not sure how I feel about your staying with me," she said, waiting for him to beg her forgiveness, to be contrite, waiting for him to just plead—if only just a little—and give her some justification for her weakness, for her inevitable capitulation.

"Maybe you should find your own place until we see how things work out for us."

He turned, facing her, his eyes opening slowly, as if squinting to bright light.

"That's OK, honey, sure. Take your time and figure things out, I'll crash somewhere."

He had picked up a few endearments along the way, "honey," "sugar," "darling," which she first thought were absurd, old-fashioned words from another time's sensibility, patronizing even. But there was unmistakable tenderness and focus on her in his speaking them, as when he called her Red, the first day they met.

"Well, there's no rush," she said. "Stay a few days."

"I'll take a look at that idea," he said.

"Stay until you get settled."

He stayed until he got settled to leave, three months later, for Paris, for the revolutionary energy bursting there, even though it was five years too late to join the barricades of '68.

"The whole thing started with the French two hundred years ago," he said. "They have it waiting in their blood to turn the whole thing over again, this time for good."

Besides, Jean Pierre was back in Paris and had promised to show him the city and to introduce him to a world of brilliant people, the future of Europe. He would never see Paris in this way were he to go alone—or even with her—and dependent on guidebooks and good luck and phone numbers of friends' friends.

He had not told her he was leaving or was thinking about it; one day he started teaching himself French from books and tapes, spending hours at his study while she went to her graduate classes and buried herself in the library. At night he worked in a West Village bar famous for the poets who had drunk there decades ago and whose reckless aura still drew the young. She came to the bar one evening at eleven and found him talking to two students she had seen at university lectures.

He was leaning over the counter and they were bent toward him on their stools; other customers waited impatiently in a crush.

He was, she heard as she drew near, speaking in French—with an accent better than her own, she who had studied the language in high school and college—haltingly but clearly and even with a certain flair, a certain gesture of the hands and lifting of the shoulders, and one of the two women was guiding him along, filling in a word now and then. Then they all laughed, the two leaving arm in arm—she could see the young woman was beautiful, in that composed French way—as Rex called out his goodbyes, *"A tout à l'heure. A la prochaine."*

Some weeks later, when she came home from the library (after a day in the stacks reading Emerson in her carrel, the transcendental brightness that came from his pages, shining, she thought—and thought one day to prove—in the vistas of the early American landscape painters), she found Rex sitting quietly at the end of the bed, smoking, blowing, as her father had done to amuse her when she was a child, old-fashioned smoke rings.

He was so odd there, alone, with his cigarette and the fat zeros crumbling in the air. It was also wonderful to see him home at so unusual an hour, the unexpected miracle of his presence, his smile.

He had even dressed himself smartly for her—like a young man on a date—his immaculate white shirt buttoned to the top, his usually wild hair now wetted and combed down. It was elegant, his being there, waiting for her, to surprise her and take her to bed in a most unroutine way, and at the cost of his evening's pay.

"Didn't you go to work tonight?" she asked. Wanting him

to say and to act on his saying, "I thought I'd take it off to be with you."

"Well, I've quit," he said. "Kinda sudden."

"Oh!" The fear came seconds before the exclamation, arriving when he had ground his cigarette out and narrowed his eyes.

"Because I'm leaving for a little while, Red."

"Leave the keys on the way out," she said.

"There you go," he said. "It's not forever. I'm just going over to Paris for a while."

"Send me a card," she said, turning to leave—to go where?

She was already home, which she knew would never feel the same again now that he had soiled it with his leaving, his smoke rings forever tumbling in air. To go where? To the library again? To the bookish walls and warmth of its lair where, of all the places in the world, she was secure.

"You could come, too, if you weren't in school."

It was funny the way he had said it, "in school," as if she were nine in pigtails, in a blue uniform with her knees naked above the long woolen socks. What a wonderful way he had of reducing her, and therefore her clarity and her dreams. Did he study how to do that in the same concentrated way he had studied French?

Years later, she was sure, so many years later that she could envision herself made calm by time and when all her unhappiness was evened out in the great wash of experience, she would recall this occasion as if it had occurred to someone other than herself. Indeed, the truth was she would be some other self.

How hard, she would say in that future moment of wisdom,

for the young to understand how time and experience flatten out all pain, how even one's suffering finds—if not purpose—some balance and redress in experience yet to be had.

She would test that truth one day, but for now she felt only the unclean severing of the other self, watching that self detach from the remaining tendons and exit by the door.

# CHAPTER 7

S HE WAS NO longer young and could not cling to the idea that her longing for Rex was a phase of youth. At thirty-five she did not consider herself old, or wise either. Stupid and adolescent and worse: infantile. She had told herself that many times; and was told that many times over her adult years in language both couched and direct by three therapists and one analyst. But she found useless and time-wasting her sorties at change, at the self-understanding that would supposedly promote transformation.

She had been to blame, of course. She resisted change, stubbornly, as do children, and so she was stuck with herself, with the damage to her life that would be repaired if she only accepted—and enacted—the reality of mature love with its acceptance of boundaries without ecstatic pleasures. But what was life without ecstatic pleasure—without Rex?

The day was long and could not accommodate passion at every hour. How little, one doctor noted, among all the activities and duties—and even pleasures—of the day, is actually taken up by love.

Her love for Rex was not love, another doctor had emphasized, but an addiction, which must be dealt with therapeutically: cold turkey and with much devotion to work. The old—and one day she, too, would be old—do not burn, and she would be grateful for the mature, nurturing love that lasts beyond youth. It was her life, not the advice, that was implausible.

As for the work part of the remedy, after she had worked hard to earn her doctorate in art history she worked even harder as a member of the faculty, having taken on additional teaching loads, joined more committees, directed more theses, juried more awards, and written more articles than any colleagues of her generation. She had been a whiz of activity, of productivity, the young, tenured associate professor at thirty, star of the department, a paragon of the university.

In an effort to change, to grow, to extend her curiosity and not get stuck in the academic mud, she had moved her area of interest from Spanish painting and Goya in particular to Poussin, for her an artist of greater formal and intellectual complexity, greater mystery, though lacking in warmth and perhaps—a word Professor Morin was fond of and one generally missing in the art historical vocabulary—wisdom. Poussin took her to France and to learning to speak excellent French, the language whose mastery, for her and her generation of scholars, was a sign of civilization with all its implied refinements of thought and comportment.

After several of her first protracted stays in Paris, her friends had found her altered, meaning that they did not always like the changes they saw in her clothes and manner. She was now saying "Excuse me" if she stepped before someone in an elevator and, when she was of a different opinion, instead of saying "You're wrong" or "Bullshit" in the direct and seemingly honest fashion of American artists and intellectuals of her time, she prefaced her disagreement with a polite "Forgive me" or "If you don't mind, may I say."

It was not exactly that she had put on airs, they thought, but that she was different, smart, very trim and composed from shoes to blouse and tailored jacket. Her hair was cut in Paris, where it had been shaped from a craggy Maine landscape to a formal eighteenth-century French garden, nature tamed and ordered—a wild thicket trimmed to a red hedge. Her skin looked tighter, her body firmer than when she had left America, and her erect carriage announced a newly acquired self-possession.

In her friends' eyes, she was, in a word at once praising and pejorative, *chic*.

After he had not seen her for a summer, Professor Morin, impeccably correct on all professional occasions when they met, looked her up and down as she approached him standing with some colleagues and exclaimed, "*Ravissante*, Dominique."

"Your beautiful *serviette*, I mean," he said, trying to cover his embarrassment.

"If I'd known you'd like it, I would have bought you one in Paris," she said, laughing.

Now she and Professor Morin spoke French together when they were alone or at dinner together. It made him feel, he said, as if he were a young man in Paris again before the Nazi occupation, when he sat in cafés with his friends and happily wasted the nights in talk. Not that their conversation was a waste, he added.

At least not for her, she said. But she knew what he had

meant. No time with him, not even time spent in chattering about the classic film noir movies they loved, was time wasted, she felt. In his presence, she was part of a rare world, where ideas were waiting to be plucked from space.

As far as the professional front was concerned, her therapists need not have worried, and as for the mature love part of their homilies, she had been working on that, as well.

The astronomer had resurfaced and was now a professor of astrophysics. Invisible holes in space that caved in on themselves and sucked up light were his specialty. She found his subject fascinating in itself but also because it proved to her that nature, including the human heart, was unknowable and mysterious. He was neither. But she tried to overlook that lack and live with what was best in him, his steadfastness and intelligence.

Unlike in their college days, he now understood how to keep her interested in him, and that while sex was not his best suit, his learning was. She found him attractive. She could enjoy looking at him across a dinner table or waking up with him in bed on Sundays on those occasions he came to stay the night at her flat and saying "Good morning, Glen," and kiss him on the cheek before going to get the *New York Times* outside her door. But she did not ever feel a lightness or a sudden rush of blood in her chest when, after not seeing him for a day or even a week, he entered a room or came through the door to join her at a restaurant table.

He was devoted to his work. Devoted to the two children from a previous marriage, who lived with their mother in Riverdale, and, she would have said, were it not for the smug thing it sounded, devoted to her. She wished less so, finding it

claustrophobic and unengaging, as she did all excessive attention. Still, he was a rational candidate for marriage, if that was
what she wanted.

They had summers off, when they could travel—the three
reasons for teaching, Glen said, were June, July, and August—
they earned reasonable incomes and could afford, by combin-
ing them, to rent a two-bedroom apartment in Manhattan, and
their friends—who praised them as a couple—mixed easily.
They seemed to fit, and in her mind they did. He asked her to
marry him. She said she would give it thought. She was still
giving it thought when, five years after he had asked, she went
to the hospital with cancer.

The left lung. A spot under the X-ray. First the operation,
then the treatment. The afternoon before the surgery and
some hours before Glen was scheduled to visit, Rex showed
up, having learned from Rose that she was going to the hospital. He had taken a plane from Paris, with what money she
could not guess. Although he had written her several times
over the past years, she had not seen him.  And as an exercise
in trying her restraint, she often did not answer her letters. She
found she missed him more when she did not. Seeing him now
thrilled her, made her more than ever want to live, made her
less afraid of dying and more afraid of never seeing him again.

"Don't leave me, Red," he said, sitting in the chair against
the light, his hair in flames.

He had come to comfort and bolster her but she was the
one who now had to come to his aid.

"How can I ever?" she said.

# CHAPTER 8

S HE WENT TO see him in Tangiers, where they stayed at
the floppy old Hôtel Villa de France, in the room where—
it was said—Matisse had lived, painting the trees and archway
to the market beneath his window. Rex had found a job teaching English at the American School, though she did not understand how he qualified without his college degree.

They had corresponded several times over the first year of
her recuperation, when he was still living in Paris. He was coming to visit her, he had written several times, but each time he
did not appear. Something urgent had come up at the last
hour—once he phoned to say that his papers were not in order
and he was afraid that if he left he would not be readmitted to
France. He asked her to be patient.

Her suitor, Glen, had been growing impatient. He had
waited a long time for her to decide to marry him—or even to
live together. Of course her illness had set things back, but
after the first year, it was clear she was on the way to full recovery, he said, so now was the time for them to move forward.

He made a joke. "Not even the stars are eternal," he said.

He had been kind to her, generous with his understanding, she said. She had not made love to him during the year since she had left the hospital, and he had assumed—and she as well—that she was physically unable to, that her body was still feeling the shock of the operation and sickening aftermaths of chemotherapy.

But when well into the second year of recovery she was still fending him off, she realized that it was not her illness but Rex's hospital visit that had turned her about and had made her long for him as never before. Death was Rex's foil, bringing him into daily relief and making her feel a new urgency—even if she did not know exactly how to translate that—to live fully every moment of her remaining life.

How could she ever better than now understand the painting she had loved from childhood or better comprehend Death's message inscribed on that Arcadian tomb—"Even in Arcadia I am"—where seemingly immortal shepherds and an immortal woman would give way to time, all vigor and beauty gone to dust? Poussin's painting, too, would one day die and go to dust: "Even in art, I am," Death might well say.

One afternoon, after receiving a letter from Rex, from Tangiers, she phoned Glen and made plans to meet him. She did not want to go to dinner or anyplace where long discussions could take place. She began talking at the top steps of the Metropolitan Museum, and at the bottom, after a slow descent, she finished. She would not marry him, live with him, sleep with him. She took his hand; she cried for him and for herself. Although she did not love him, she felt herself dying: another severance, another loss, another failure.

"I miss you, come soon," Rex wrote. He was in Tangiers when he answered her letter in which she suggested she visit him during spring recess. She imagined him writing her from an outdoor café, while drinking mint tea and blowing smoke rings, the soft O's crumbling over his head. She was meeting him on wholly new and glamorous grounds, and having erased Glen's name from the slate, she felt she could now cleanly chalk Rex's back in. She was doubtful, however, that that was all she had to do to keep it there.

She arrived in Tangiers on the day she said she would, carrying the minimum of baggage, a lean traveler. They kissed on the cheek three times, Parisian-style—dear old friends. They went to the hotel—she paid for the taxi, though he did make a fuss and grew, she thought, petulant as the bills changed hands—where she showered under a feeble drizzle, and dried off with a stale towel.

The window opened to the red jars of olives and piles of Berber carpets and mounds of spices she imagined were waiting behind the market walls and narrow streets. Wrapped in a towel, she stood at the window, her hair a damp red fire mounted on a creamy neck. She turned. He was draped on the bed, no cigarette this time. The same man almost, thin, lithe, but older about the eyes. He pulled the braided belt from his khakis and laid it beside him coiled. She felt it in her stomach, the belt waiting there, patiently, for her. He had learned new things in her absence. He smiled, slowly unzipping his fly.

She wrote, on the mornings when he went out to teach, at a little desk by the open window. For some while since her operation, and without publication its goal, she had been jotting down, without order or pattern, anecdotes gleaned from the late nineteenth and twentieth centuries, noting down those matters or events which moved her. One day these notes and fragments of thought might form a coherent mosaic and reveal to her her own spiritual autobiography as well as a biography of her time.

It was her hobby away from her academic writing, but the activity was not light—like making watercolors on vacation, as her friend Rose did. The very haphazard nature of the chronology, the arbitrariness of what she chose to write about, freed her from convention, and the immediacy—and for her, the modernity—of the material made her feel she had left behind Poussin and the seventeenth century for a while and that she was indeed living in or proximate to her own time.

She had been trained to displace herself before a work of art, to efface all personality and autobiography in the service of illuminating the work. But cancer and the sense of her living in Death had given her an authority and freedom she never before had possessed. It was time to put herself in the mix, and fasten down what she most felt and believed.

One morning she had written a passage she was tempted to read to Rex, but didn't. It was about Gauguin.

"He was dying in a jungle, impoverished and alone, in a hut of his construction, far away from everything that was his life in Europe. He had no idea if he and his paintings would be remembered. But he kept painting to the last moment, getting up from his sickbed to brush a few strokes on the canvas. On the lintel over the door to his hut he had carved the motto 'Be in love and you will always be happy.' "

When Rex returned in the afternoons, they drank a red Moroccan wine and ate black and green olives with a flat bread. It was all the meal they required in their economy of time, in their wish to shrink the world and its appetites, setting it in contrast to their hunger for each other.

They went to bed and made love and slept until the mosque's call to prayer sang through the afternoon air at five, when she woke and went back to her desk, writing while he slept or read—now he was buried in Unamuno's *Tragic Sense of Life* and Schopenhauer's *World as Will and Idea.*

The wastefulness of wanting was Rex's current theme; he wished, he said, to pare down his life and limit his desires. Not all desires, he added, smiling at her. He was finding, he said, much wisdom in Sufism, and made her a present of a line taken from the *Hadith*, or the traditions of the Prophet, "God is beautiful and loves beauty."

In the early evening they went down for mint tea at the Café de Paris, where they dawdled and read, while the sparrows rioted in the stubby trees of the boulevard. It resembled order, their day; or routine, which is the foundation of order, but she felt a chaos in her thinking, in her concentration, in her speech even. Her writing sometimes went up and down the page like little breasts without nipples.

She had welts on her ass and could not go down to the pool for a week. The red welts turned black and blue. She liked his marks and the being angry with him after he belted her. Their new phase took them from the open world and into their own secret retreat, suggesting also that all thoughts of domesticity were henceforth banished from their lives. She was free from considering him someone she might marry. For the moment, she preferred to be bitten at the neck, brought to her hands and knees, hinds in the air, beaten and fucked into submission.

She was there with him in the hotel room at night, a crescent moon in the window and a braided belt hanging between her teeth, her head down on the pillow, her ass in the air, her breasts hanging heavily and swaying each time he smacked her cheeks with the flat of his smart hand, and with each stroke of his fucking her.

The world had shut down its nervous enterprises, the responsible clocks had taken a rest, the warm breezes from the Mediterranean, however, still caressed her when she woke in the morning and fanned her after she showered and dried herself by the open window, where she could see him pass on his way to work and wave to her from the twisting street below.

"Be in love and you will always be happy," Gauguin wrote, even as Death waited for him in the palm leaves. She was in love. She wanted to be happy. She was happy.

"Rex," she said, a few days before having to return to finish the remaining weeks of the semester, "I'm thinking of coming back here and spending the summer with you."

"That's a great idea," he answered. "Only I don't know where I'll be this summer."

"Why not?" she asked, her heart pounding.

"They didn't renew my contract at the school, Dominique," he said. "I may just go back to Paris."

"I'm sorry," she said. She had only now realized from the chagrin in his voice that he had cared about his job at the school and been hurt by the firing. She liked him for not having told her earlier, for his having tried to protect her from feeling upset for him.

"Well, I can join you in Paris, then," she continued. "Or you could come back and be with me in New York."

"What would I do there?" he asked.

"What will you do in Paris?"

"We'll have to work it out," he said, after a long pause. "Let's just enjoy these next few days, OK?"

"OK," she said, feeling humiliated for having put herself where she could be—and was—brushed off, and angry with him for not having been happy with her proposal.

"OK," she repeated, her heart darkening. She held back her tears until nightfall, after he had left the hotel on some errand.

She limped along for a day, pretending to be cheerful and keyed into him, but she was growing embittered and could not face him with honest warmth. She began to catalog her resentments against him, counting among the new ones that since she had arrived he had never once asked about her writing and her work or, worse, never had inquired about her health. Yet she knew that all he had to do was beg her to be with him for the summer and she would put her resentments, new and old, behind at least for the remainder of her stay.

Finding a pretext, she took a flight a day earlier than scheduled. He accompanied her to the airport, going as far as the gate. They kissed, as they had when she arrived, on the cheeks. They embraced. He told her it had been wonderful to be with her and that they would work out a way to see one another in a while.

"Sure, Rex," she said coolly, before waving goodbye and boarding the plane.

There was a breeze blowing through Tangiers when she left and it must have been still blowing through the open window when Rex returned to find the farewell letter she had left, propped up against the bureau mirror.

She summarized crisply the bitter items in her catalog, adding his most recent wrongs. It was stupid of her, she said to write such an accounting, but she could not say it to his face without shattering everything between them, including what was and had been good, been beautiful, even. "If there was ever," she concluded, "anything between us to wait for, don't wait now."

It was she, however, who waited, hoping for a letter or phone call expressing his sadness at her leaving, his missing her, his regrets at not having made concrete plans to join her.

She was still waiting for that letter when she spied him, two years later, child on his shoulders, in the Paris park.

# CHAPTER 9

BUT ALL THE bridges had not yet fallen from the sky and all the buildings stood solidly in their usual places; the light belonged to the beautiful, happy summer and not to the sickly violet shades of a world in rubbles. She did not yet have to answer Eric's question of whether or not, when the world tumbled down leaving only them, she was lonely.

He was more attractive in the day, when he was busy and in motion—even if it was only to walk briskly to a kiosk to buy the *Herald Tribune* than at night. For that reason she liked making love to him in the afternoon. He took charge in bed, as he did when ordering a meal in a restaurant, careful that a full course was served, from appetizer to dessert. He kissed the scar on her chest, where they had opened her, he kissed her eyes. He loved her body.

She told him the truth about her age, partly from vanity, hoping he would say—as he did—"Forty? You look twenty-five," and partly because she wanted a clean slate with no later recriminations. He was thirty-six and did look twenty-five.

She liked him in bed and she liked him out on the street, where he also, but more quietly, took charge, while picking up on the boundaries of her moods and disposition. She took him to a small prints and drawings gallery, where, with patience and over time, little gems could be found. Not that she could afford even the smallest drawing.

She pulled out from a portfolio a little pencil sketch by Lhote, a minor twentieth-century French Cubist she liked for his modesty and the lyrical way he chopped his lines.

Eric came by to look over her shoulder, and caressed the base of her neck. She felt uncomfortable when lovers snuggled and petted in public, even in Paris, where it was more done than not.

She turned about abruptly to chide him, but stopped herself when she saw his tender smile, and said laughingly, "Oh! It's only you!" He must have caught something in her expression that told him she was about to be displeased, and he answered, enigmatically, she thought, "It's only me, once."

She wondered at herself and her reaction to his caress. Was she a prude? Had it been someone else—Rex say—would she have felt differently? She had been thinking about Rex ever since she spied him in the park.

"Do you like it?" she asked, setting the sketch on a table.

He studied it for a minute. "It's a bit lightweight," he said.

"It's not Picasso or Braque, but it's very good, don't you think?" she said.

"Not Juan Gris, either," he said. Letting her graciously know, she understood, that he was not entirely out of his element. "But putting it that way," he said, "I agree."

She was afraid she had given the sketch too much attention and that he would offer to purchase it for her, but he did not. He had remembered to the letter her asking him not to try to buy her by buying her expensive things—although some part of her was piqued that he had not tried.

While he took her hand as they strolled through the city and gave her his arm as she exited from a taxi later that day, he made no further attempts at public intimacy, for which she was relieved, while wishing in some crevice of herself that he had been more transgressive. She was, she thought, impossible to please when she was not in love. When she was, she'd relish the crumbs from a napkin.

They had their last dinner before his leaving for New York at the Balzar, a bistro not far from his hotel. He had proposed—and had the hotel concierge make the reservation—to go to a super place with three or four stars and she readily agreed, wanting to please him on their last night. But at the last minute he said he had changed his mind—if she didn't mind.

"It's not what you would like," he said. "And it's against the grain of how we've been spending our time together. Let's finish it all of one piece. All right?"

"Nothing could have made me like you more than this," she said, surprisingly touched. "Nothing could have been more generous of you," she said, kissing him.

That morning she helped him pack his bags, putting between two shirts an Italian silk tie she had bought for him and which he would find, with a note, when he arrived in New York. They drove to the airport in the same car that had mate-

rialized on the Ile St. Louis when they first met. They spoke
very little. They held hands. They kissed.

As he was about to go through security, he turned and said:
"I love you, Dominique."

"It's slower for me," she said, wanting to be fair and not say
words she did not fully mean. "But I'm coming to love you."

# CHAPTER 10

T HE DAY AFTER Eric left for New York her concierge brought up a small parcel. It was the Lhote sketch she had liked. He had brought off getting it to her elegantly, she thought, and admired him even more.

That afternoon she went to the Parc Montsouris to read, she told herself, but there were other reasons for going there that she did not wish to acknowledge. It was, she reasoned, a better park for reading than the Luxembourg, because, for an American, the Luxembourg was the extended terrace of the Café Flor, and there she might run into someone she knew who would distract her complicity with the page.

The Parc Montsouris was green and quiet and out of the way of distracting tourist traffic, but after three days of sitting there in quietude from ten to five she went to the Luxembourg, where the leaves did not molt the page and cause her to look up every few moments to adjust her eyes to the light. Look out into the traffic of children and parents and students and all kinds of folks with lives, none of whom she remotely recognized.

She sat in the Luxembourg three more days, moving from

the café area to the circle above the central pond, to the area below where children plied their schooners, to the Rue de Fleurus side of the park not far from the donkey cart and pony rides, and then finally to the children's section with its skyward swings and downward slides and creamy beige sandboxes where, somewhere in their midst, stood Rex.

"Hello, Dominique," he said. "I was hoping you'd turn up."

"Turn up," as if he had known she was in Paris. He was too casual about seeing her come out of nowhere and she suspected he had spied her in the park earlier.

"Hello yourself, Rex."

"The little partner here is Kenji," he said, lifting the child up to the Paris sky.

"Dat," the boy said, his index finger pointing to a sparrow overhead.

"Is he the Buddha?" she asked. So heartbreakingly beautiful was he, so serene, with wisps of red hair twirling in the blue.

"Something of the sort; he's my teacher, anyway," Rex said with a smile she had never before seen.

They walked in silence across the park to the top of Boulevard Montparnasse, and then to the Metro station, the boy looking and pointing at her, Rex doing a little trot from time to time, the pony to the child. She followed them down into the Metro. When they got to the turnstile, he said, "Come on an' squeeze through on my ticket."

She did not mean to follow him but she found herself pushing through as he had asked, entering the train and sitting beside him and the boy, feeling, oddly enough, that they were a family on the way home from a day in the park. Indeed, they were on the way home, to Rex's flat in the working-class suburb of St. Denis, where it was as gray and chilly as Paris had been blue and mild. A proletarian climate to match the proletarian rent.

The flat was two flights above a murky café, already at six lit with a greenish fluorescence. A fluorescence that floated upward to bathe the small living room in acid greenness. A brown leather chair with one leg half broken and buoyed up by a crutch of books, a white cot with square red pillows against the wall for a couch, and, by the window, a table and lamp, whose light carved a soft white silhouette in the green window.

"Here we are," he said.

He removed the child's clothes and bathed him in a large plastic bassinet with warm water drawn from the kitchen sink, dried and powdered and re-dressed him in blue pajamas coated with stars.

The boy pointed at Dominique: "Dat," he said. "Dat."

He was one and three months and she took him in her arms feeling the feathery weight of his life. He poked his finger in her mouth and smiled.

"Oh!" she exclaimed. "Isn't he the little prince," she said, returning the boy.

"He's the one," Rex said. "He's the whole thing itself."

She looked about again. An orange curtain opened to a bed heaped with books and soiled laundry, socks dangling at the bed's edge. She had glimpsed a toilet on the landing; there was no bath or shower, she feared. Disgusting.

"And the mother?" she asked, feeling for the first time since their meeting in the park that this was a Rex of another life. That he was, finally, without her, or actually, she without him.

Feeling, too, that if she had had a son with Rex—she who had not wanted children—she would not have craved her own child as much as this rare one. There are a lack of affinities everywhere, even for those that are born from our body. How much more proof did she need that life's choices were minted in heaven, even though at the same time, she refused to believe so.

"She's dead," he said.

She sat at the edge of the cot and studied her shoes, which had felt tissue-light that morning and were now anvils anchoring her feet to the bruised wooden floor.

"And me?" she asked, the words rushing from her without filter. "Am I dead, too? Did you grieve for me these years without me?"

"Now, Dominique," he said, "go easy in front of Kenji here."

Kenji's expression had changed, a look of fearful surprise came over him, setting him to the edge of tears. She moved to hold him but he drew away.

She lowered her voice but could not give up her anger. "Why aren't you dead, Rex?"

He shrugged.

"Maybe you are, you bad ghost." She knew it was silly what she said, like a child reaching out to hurt but not yet having the language for it. "Bad ghost," she repeated.

Rex laughed, and finally, looking at him and at the child now smiling again, she did, too. Rex gave her the boy to hold, while he disappeared behind the curtain. The child looked up at her sweetly.

"Mum ma," he said. And then, with a look collapsing the world down to just her—and which made her feel weighted with longing for him—"Coo kie."

His skin was smooth, lemon-yellow and blushed red at the

cheeks. There must be millions like him, little Japanese boys with red hair and a golden smile. Millions. But she had not known any, and never seen one like him. Perhaps because all children had been the same to her, her friends' children most of all. Some were more agreeable than others, but she never felt their pull or the magnetic chemistry of motherhood. Intelligent women becoming senseless, going predictably bourgeois, exchanging sexuality for dreary motherhood; bottles and diapers and rattles, rooms smelling of shit and urine, women's conversation and their brains—and their bodies—turned to pabulum.

She was not made for children and the servitude that went with them. Neither was Rex, she had thought. To raise them all those years only to have them leave; to sacrifice vital years of reading and travel and sex just to make more of what was already in abundance. Finally, whatever her justification, she never felt the longing for children except now, with this Kenji falling asleep in her arms. Not to have children, but to have him.

Rex returned with two glasses of red wine and sat himself down in the crippled chair and started speaking. She was not paying attention, her mind surveying the disgusting room she would have washed and scrubbed and polished and made sparkle and shine as she would the windows, shine brightly even in the sootiest day, the disgusting room that she'd make smell of ocean and roses.

Rex talked, the words curling about the room. It grew darker. Still talking, he fed the boy and placed him in a crib standing before her eyes. She felt far from his words and she was growing tired, the lateness probing her bones.

She asked him to call a taxi. They were hard to get in these outlying districts, Rex said. She could take the cot and he'd bunk on the floor, if she wanted. She just wanted to be away from him and to fall into sleep for a few centuries and wake up never remembering she had met him again, remembering only the boy, "Dat."

Finally, Rex went down to the café and found a man with a blue Citroën willing to take her home for some little money, a thin Moroccan with a pencil mustache. The car was his cousin's, Ali explained as he drove away, a car that Rex borrowed from time to time—they were all a family in that quarter. Fez was once a great center of learning in the ancient world, did she know that? Yes, she did.

And did she know that Rex was a powerful man, with much *baraka*, much power, he said. She had heard such rumors, she said, but she did not know that aspect of him well enough to confirm them. What was the nature of this power? she asked.

It was not anything that he did; it was his fiber, very closely woven and impermeable. "His basket holds," the Moroccan said. He would make a very good Muslim, he added. A very clear man, yes. Rex was a man very clear to God.

# CHAPTER II

THE PHONE RANG dully under a red pillow. She let it grind the air for a minute before deciding that whoever was signaling her from the other end of the wire would not give up. It could not be Rex, so there was no reason to answer. There was no reason, in any case, were it he. In any case, again, he did not have her number, or know where she lived. His curiosity ended at the tip of his nose. Not true, of course. At the end of his prick. Not true, again.

She made a pot of coffee and returned to her desk. The ringing had ceased or had blended into the silence somewhere along the way, because now she had withdrawn, however fitfully, into her book—if that's what it was, this book on Poussin that was taking forever and needed five forevers more to cohere. Her book, where, when she immersed herself in it, all worry disappeared.

She was trying to understand why Poussin had shifted so radically from his expansive, colorful Italianate period to a style severe and restrained, every form in balance, and with a minimum of color, and that muted. The new work had been described as Classical, as if it followed a formula for pictorial unity and composition.

There were historical reasons for Poussin's shift to austere Classicism, when the prevailing mode was Baroque flamboyancy, but she suspected others. One especially, for which she had no empirical evidence and which she dare not publish for fear of ridicule—though she wrote the chapter anyway.

Certain artists, she believed, no matter what their time in history, have a perception of Plato's irreducible, Ideal forms and express that perception in ways recognizable to other artists of their own and of later times. The fourteenth-century Italian Giotto had that vision, the seventeenth-century Poussin, too, and Cézanne, who followed him and who, she wrote, near the end of his life went to the Louvre and made two copies of *The Arcadian Shepherds*.

What did Cézanne see in Poussin if not the foreshadowing of all he was doing by reducing nature to cones and spheres and planes and thus echoing their archetypes in the world of Ideas? She planned to make the same case for Picasso's Platonic perceptions in his Cubist and Classical periods, were she ever to get that far in her book.

Once, years earlier, when she tried explaining to Glen her ideas on Poussin's move to painting's formal unity, which she thought were born from the artist's Platonic intimations, he politely scoffed at the idea. How, he asked, in the chaos and randomness of the universe, could she imagine anything so unfeasible as a dominant and underlying order of forms? She had no answer, only the surety of her feelings—her own intuition and perception of such an order, in art and, she did not tell him this, in love.

One hour later she had burned down five Gitanes—

disobeying her doctor's injunction that she never smoke again—and had written three paragraphs. She was on the road to another when the buzzer buzzed.

Flowers. The concierge held a bouquet obscuring her head; more white roses soaked in pails at her feet. From Eric, naturally. Notes with each bouquet. One read: "New York is barren without you." Not inspired, but sweet, she thought. Another, and to her more winning in its simplicity: "I miss you." Everything was in good taste except for the gross amount of flowers themselves—if three are good, why not two hundred?

Rex would have brought her a single rose, and even if it had been one he had found dying in the trash, it would have been beautiful, in its last ripeness. A rose of no purpose, celebrating no event or holiday, asking no favor, but speaking to her for Rex and the beauty of their love. But that was long ago.

In brief, and brought down to their simple function, the flowers heralded Eric's intention to return—were she amenable—to Paris, to her. He missed her, and missed Paris, too, but only as it was her terrain, and thus he would meet her in Paris or anywhere she wished. He did not say "I love you" or sign off "with love," which was all to the good, showing some distinction and the intelligence not to drain words of their blood.

The morning's writing now interrupted, so too was her concentration and her good intentions to give the day wholly to her work, and thus to herself. The days were slipping by and soon she would have to return to America and to her teaching, to everything agreeable, congenial, and, finally, without fire.

She considered returning to work, interruption or no, but the idea seemed part of another day far gone and of one still to come. She lacked discipline, unlike Rex, who, as when he decided to learn French, was all vagrant discipline but with nothing creative to apply it to except doing tasks. He had more discipline and perhaps more self-assurance than she, yet neither virtue yielded anything of value to himself or to others, and thus she was superior morally, intellectually, and, when it came down to it, she was elevated in every way—so that she had the right to leave her work and wander for a few hours, the right to waste the day down to its nub should she choose.

Book in hand, she went down to her café, where she found Rex at a table in seeming conversation with his son. The Moroccan had told him her street but had not remembered the building number, Rex explained.

"Kenji said that if we waited here long enough you'd show up."

"Was it his idea that you look for me?"

"No, but he wanted to come along."

"I'm glad he did," she said, lifting him from his chair and taking him in her arms. He poked at her mouth, urging a crust of bread into it.

"Mum ma," he said.

"He's taking my heart away," Dominique said, laughing.

"That'll make things happier," he said. "When you come live with us."

She first thought to make light of him and his presumption. Instead, she ordered a *crème* and two croissants; one for the boy, who was now studying her placidly, his black eyes banishing all her mean thoughts.

"Sure," she said finally to the cup, "I'll just go and pack my bags and we're off *chez toi.*"

*"Chez nous,"* he corrected.

The boy pulled the croissant to shreds, eating from time to time the pieces that had fallen to the plate and table. "Coo kie," he said, pointing to the shreds and pushing some toward her.

*"Chez moi,"* she said. "I'll take him with me and leave you to yourself, where you're best left."

"His mother liked croissants, too, one of the few things Western she allowed for."

"Except for you," Dominique said.

"She didn't much allow for me either, she just fucked me one night out of pride."

"I'm leaving," Dominique said. "I just came down for a coffee, and now I've had one. To stay for two is redundant, as is talking to you."

"You sure do talk fancy. Doesn't she, Kenji?"

The boy agreed, nodding his head and smiling. But he did the same when she asked him if his dad wasn't the most silly man in the world.

She rose and kissed the boy on his head. Rex took her arm as she turned to leave.

"There's nothing but us and never will be," he said.

"Maybe," she said, softening. "But we're a shipwreck."

"We'll fix it," he said earnestly.

His eyes turned colors, she imagined, from slate green to bright blue, his red hair seemed to burst into orange flames.

"You're a kind of chameleon, Rex. You change complexion to suit the mood. I never knew you had that skill."

"That's just psychic chemistry. It's nothing you learn, Dominique."

The sea swelled and sunk, a decade or more ago, the boat

drifting and swelling and sinking and sliding, with Rex curled up sleeping in the stern, a beautiful young man, still pure, still clear and unblotched by experience.

Now, in his café chair, child in his lap, he was a Rex somewhat worn by life, with what disappointments she did not know—and swore not to care—and on the path to a middle age empty of promise and filled with regrets. Or was that her own life she saw so clearly sitting before her?

"If I could only shake you," she said, "and get you to see the ridiculous fake you are. While there's still a chance, I wish I could do it."

She left him, his head down and somber in his chair, the boy looking after her, an expression of surprise and sadness on his face. For a moment she thought of turning back but a sense of power surged in her and she continued down the street to her flat. So much for that, once and forever finished. It was easy.

Once home she phoned Eric in New York and left a message on his answering machine saying that he should come to Paris at the end of the following week, saying also that the flowers were lovely and that she was keeping three and sending the rest to a nearby hospital. Not true, but he'd get the point.

She went back to work. To write a longish sentence. Which she then revised. Then rewrote. Then deleted. Then panicked at the loss and struggled to write the original sentence whole from memory. Then she rose from her desk and rushed back down to the café, where Rex was still sitting and Kenji was drawing circles in the air. Like Raphael, she thought, perfect circles by hand.

"And what if I come with you, then what?" she asked. The

question to which there was no real answer, but she had not posed it expecting one.

Ali's blue car was parked just around the corner, and Ali himself was in it behind the wheel, smiling as he greeted them. When they arrived, he got out and opened the door, making a little bow to Kenji and father, and a salaam—I am yours, heart, words, mind—to Dominique.

Nods to Rex from five unshaven men drinking mint tea at the café terrace. They looked her up and down then went back to their tea. She had been sorted out and weighed on the scale of value. *A Thousand and One Nights* replayed; she, the Scheherazade come to St. Denis's harem. Ali and the blue Citroën quickly disappeared, the genie and his flying carpet away in a whisk.

And now she was upstairs in the seraglio of one, ruled by a child prince and an impoverished sultan. She looked to the window for escape. It was not barred. The apartment was cleaner, less cluttered than the previous night, the windows shone and a pot of irises spun a bluish veil on the table. She turned to speak but didn't. They kissed. Then for the third time. She could feel Kenji's stare, although each time she stopped to look he was turned away, seated on the floor stabbing a red pencil into a large white pad.

She was kissing Rex again when someone knocked at the door. Ali, with a gift of dried fruit, come to take Kenji away for the afternoon, to his cousin's two floors above, where they loved him very much and tended him while Rex was away. Was Rex going away, she asked, after Ali withdrew, child in arm.

Yes, they were both going away to the room behind the orange curtain, to the bed that camped in it. It was so familiar, his body, his moves. They slept some while and woke and made love again. They had done the same an hour earlier, a day earlier, every day of their life for the past hundred and one years.

At dusk, the greenish light from the café below echoed through the room.

"The green hour," she said, "*l'heure verte*, called so because in the early evening everyone in Paris went to the cafés to drown themselves in milky green absinthe. Did you know that, Rex?"

"Sort of, Red."

"In the cafés," she continued, "in the 1890s, before it was illegal to drink absinthe."

"What beautiful times they must have been," he said.

"I'm surprised you'd think that. The art was great and life was great for the rich, the rest were in the pits."

"The class struggle was very clear then; it's better covered now," he said.

That sounded so funny, "the class struggle," so far away from the world in which she now lived, a concept from their youth.

"Are you still involved with that Lefty stuff?" she asked, dreading that in their years apart little had matured in his thoughts.

"I'm not," he answered. "But that doesn't mean that capitalism has gotten any kinder than when people were sipping that green juice in cafés."

"The awful everywhere in triumph," she said. "As always."

"Don't let it get you down, Red, at least not today," he said. His eyes sparkled.

As a joke, she began to hum "The Internationale."

"Hey! That's my song," he said. "I sang it when I was a boy."

Sang it when he was a wild boy who dived from masts, but now he was a strangely reassuring and certain man, with his child upstairs occupying the neighbors and him calmly saying that soon he had to leave for work and would come home hoping to find her.

"To work? And where is that?" she asked, looking at the three-legged chair, the bureau in splintered veneer, the standing iron lamp bandaged at the base with gray electrical tape, the holes in the salmon shade, also patched with the same gray tape, the piles of washed shirts and kid's clothes, the ambient green lighting.

All this time, he had been living in France illegally, without papers. But he had found a job in a shop repairing and maintaining expensive racing bikes—the French being passionate about a good *bicyclette*, mad for racing them. He had become something of a wizard at his profession, sought after by the serious bikers who brought their wheels from everywhere in France—and Belgium—just to be in his care.

He said all that proudly, as one would say of himself he was a brain surgeon or astrophysicist or a professor of art history, published and recognized by her peers, even if they disagreed with her, had found her thinking elitist, out of fashion, dead. Of course, there was more to his bike repair story, she was certain.

After some prodding, he admitted that one day he wanted to build his own bikes from scratch, to make each a work of uniqueness and beauty—and speed. Like a great sculpture, he said, a sculpture that unites, as does no other construction, person and machine—a car does not realize that without the intermediary of fuel, the necessary and separating third party.

Had he ever read *The Third Policeman*, she asked, the novel which proposes that the atoms of a bike merge with that of its rider, creating a hybrid of manbike and bikeman in the exchange? No, he had never read that book, reading mostly, these days, technical books relating to his profession. He did not say profession. His *métier*, he said, as would some French cab driver or waiter speaking of his trade.

She wanted to shower, but there was none. A tub. He volunteered to make a shower stall for her when she came to live with them, a sprinkler on a pole, for her.

He was dressing. Blue T-shirt and blue coveralls and thick-soled, low boots neither black nor brown but a silvery mud, and thick wool red socks. He combed his hair slick back with water, a feature of his toilette which he had first assumed on his leaving her for Paris.

He had come between her breasts and now she was still sticky and wanted to wash, but he asked her not to.

"Don't wash," he said. "At least until I return."

She laughed.

"Please," he said. "I want me sticking to you, glued to you."

He was at the door, his favorite location after the bed. They kissed, then a few times more, very deeply, like young people in love. He asked her to stay, to wait for him to return. She promised she would consider it.

"If not, come back the next day," he said at the door. "But do come back soon, you hear?"

He had said the same some lives ago when they were sailing the romantic seas.

She went upstairs and found the boy seated on the floor with two women and Ali surrounding him. They were not surprised to see her, and nodded when she entered the room as if she had been in their lives forever. The boy looked up at her and smiled, the index finger of his right hand pointing to the ceiling, to heaven, to the great Muslim oasis in the next life.

The grown ones were smiling, a great contentment had seemingly come over them, now that she had arrived.

*"Il est très philosophe,"* the older of the two women said, nodding to the boy.

*"Comme son papa,"* the other added.

# CHAPTER 12

WHAT WOULD SHE say of her life? That on the whole it was a good life, that she wished it were longer. That it took a lifetime to learn how to live, but by then only a few wintry years remained to apply the knowledge. We all need two lives, one to learn how to live, the other to live it.

So, what *would* she say of her life? Only, and finally with any certainty, that in spite of all understanding of its senselessness, she wanted more life and more at its earlier side, when the page was just half written. A life with Rex at twenty-five, instead of forty. A life forever at twenty-five, remaining fixed there in youth, and in love.

Then one would not need two lives and one would not fear mistakes or disastrous choices that consumed irreplaceable and finite time. Then one would need learn nothing and living would include—and erase—all errors and all loss as part of the refundable day; the day but not any regrettable choice, repeating itself.

When she was nineteen, she went to swim in an ocean cove, where she could see her parents' simple saltbox house high on the cliffs. Then she closed her eyes to house and cliff and sky and stayed floating on her back. It was eleven, the sun was warm but not yet fierce. She was topless and the water lapped at her breasts and nipples in long soft swells, her body, neither warm nor cold, swaying gently in the sea's wet cradle. An animal in optimum health and spiritual stasis. No thoughts, no hopes, no fears, no hungers whatsoever. What did it matter if the rest of her life was lived in that floating state? Never to read or see paintings or make love again—all that was so wonderfully far away and for another life.

It would have been the perfect moment to die. The lesson was so clear but she missed it then, as indeed did the whole of the deluded world every day. All extensions in time beyond the perfect moment of contentment begged for trouble. All that followed that great moment was the diminishment of self and the substitution of animal joy with ambition and accomplishments.

And what of memory? In her scheme, would memory of the previous day attach itself to the new dawn? Would she carry the wound of Rex's leaving her on a Monday when, on the following day, a new Monday surfaced with the sun? A life of blank Mondays.

So that when she went upstairs and saw Kenji point to the ceiling, implying to her the dome of the universe and to some message inscribed to her there, and had felt her heart filled with the boy's inexplicable serenity, did she think of staying and completing the family? She did. Thought it several times, with many pictures of a world narrowed down to just three, until finally, and without a thought, she asked Ali to take her home.

The car, he said sadly, was broken, so why didn't she stay?

She could have called a taxi or walked down to the street and found one or gone down to the nearest Metro—no matter how far it was—and ridden home. Another day in the life of Dominique and Rex concluded.

She looked again at the boy: His smile brightened the room, the city. He ran to her, offering his open palm, a little ball of couscous at its center. A plate of it rested on the floor where he had been eating. When she bent to kiss him, he pressed the food to her lips.

"Dat," he said.

His was not a deep chest of words but he did not need many to win her. She lifted him up and kissed him, and after some exchanges with the trio of guardians, took him down to his father's apartment, where she stayed playing and tending to him until Rex's return.

# CHAPTER 13

S HE ARRANGED A hasty leave of absence from the
 university on the contingence of extending her research
in Paris. As usual, Professor Morin had helped smooth the way
with the administration, vouching for the importance of her
work. She had phoned him at his apartment, when it was ten
a.m. in New York, still too early for him; he usually went to
bed at three or four in the morning after having spent the
night reading in a sagging armchair she had always asked him
to upholster or junk.

"I'm staying in Paris with Rex," she said bluntly. "But I'm
also trying to finish my Poussin book," she added, not wanting
to make her request for his help wholly a personal matter.

She was nervous on the phone, rattling her information.
When she was a child, her parents used the phone sparingly
and then only for local use; a call to someone up island in
Riverhead they deemed long-distance, subject to high rates per
minute—and then there were the taxes.

"I'll write you everything, Samuel," she said.

"Don't waste the time," he answered. "What is there any-more to know? Just tell me you're well."

"I'm well," she said. "Maybe I'm crazy, but I'm well."

"I give you a big hug," he said. "A big hug," then rang off.

She met with Eric one afternoon in the Palais Royal gar-dens after he had been waiting two days practically at her doorstep. She had nearly forgotten him and her call asking him to come to her in Paris. She did not tell him that. She was pleased to see him, in a vague way. The reading under the trees, the Buttes-Chaumont, where she got tipsy and even a little sen-timental, all gauzy and removed from the larger moment. But with the romantic patina gone, their separation and recent events had transformed him from a lover to an old friend on a visit to Paris.

He was gracious enough not to press her, but he was visibly angry that he had come all that way not to find her waiting, not to have her return his calls, forced to cool his heels while wor-rying where she was, only to find she was not in the hospital, not in the morgue, not anywhere—from his point of view—unpleasant.

Baby-sitting a friend's child, she explained. True enough, but so stupid-sounding, so dismissive of him, finally, that she soon told him the truth and the little history of her life with Rex. She told it quickly, without too many asides into the deeper realm of her feelings. There was this fellow student she had loved and still loved, all these years after, and after many separations and reunions and disappointments: the usual love story; the result, however, was that she had found it difficult to love anyone else—or to love anyone else for very long.

Of course, she liked him and had had hopes of knowing him better or perhaps of even coming to love him, until the accident of seeing Rex and his son in the park after some years of their last—what could she call it—partnership, union, cohabitation. None of the words would do, but they would serve, she supposed.

It was Indian summer but the light traveled like deep fall, obliquely, and washed the warm yellow sky with translucent sheets of bluish slate. As in the illumination in Poussin's paintings; an unnatural light meant to express the ineffable atmosphere of timelessness, even as the day dove into shadow and death.

She was in fact not sure of what Poussin had intended by that light, but in her writing she had matched it to what she considered *The Arcadian Shepherds'* theme: the omnipresence of Death in the center of life. She believed that every centimeter of a painting—every color, line, image—bore an explicable relation to another, whether the artist had intended or had understood the relationship or not. A great artist, that is. That qualification was unstated but assumed by art historians. But, then, what made an artist great? That he made great paintings, of course. A tautology that led nowhere.

All criticism was a form of fiction and consensus, a certain agreement made for a period and time, and after that the verdict could change and often did change. Every generation made its own judgments; none were immutable. Let the painting not the artist speak, she had concluded after years of study and writing, but by the time she had left some impress to that effect on critical thought, her world had changed and she and some kindred others were drifting on an open boat some way from the fashionable mainland. Now she sailed with the retrograde crew.

Poussin's light was bathing them in the park and was sounding their theme. Not so much that they were dying, although that was true enough, since everything alive was doing the same, but that their future had died. Eric was sad. There was nothing that he could do to change her feelings or their situation; he was realistic enough to understand that and not to try. He said that he understood, in any case. But he added more as the afternoon wound down to coffee and a long stroll in her apartment's direction: He took her hand unexpectedly and kissed it with the dreamy fervor of an uxorious husband leaving for a long voyage.

He stood very tall, addressing her as she imagined he would a board meeting or a collection of shareholders—not that she knew what either looked like—and explained his position, as he called it. He looked distinguished during his recitation, and for a moment she liked him again, remembering even why she had found him attractive to begin with.

He would be her friend; they would be friends, he hoped. Who knows what might happen for them both in the years to come; in the meantime, they both had much to do; he did, in any event. But he was sure that some part of him would always love her—or at least always like her, he added, laughing.

She smiled and said she liked constancy, she was a fool for it. And she thought of a letter Poussin had written to a friend and which had always made her feel a kinship with him. "I'm not fickle or changing in my affection once I have given it to a person," he wrote, speaking for her now centuries earlier.

"Of course we'll stay friends," she said. "But with time you'll see your other feelings will change, Eric. Everything does."

"But the point, Dominique, is that you never change," he said.

It struck her how obvious a point it was, and how true.

# CHAPTER 14

S UCH BEAUTIFUL DAYS: She understood that even
while she was living them. Even when the day was most
ordinary, a day passing like any other, if ever there was such a
thing, she knew to be grateful. And she was.

When Rex came home at night, a smudge of machine oil
still on his washed hands and neck—the aroma of metal
spokes and rubber tires in his hair—and Kenji ran to him, and
Rex lifted him up in the air, kissing him, and held her tightly
about her waist with his free arm, did she not kiss him and say:
"I'm happy"? She did. For all her high-minded thoughts, she
was a simpleton of pleasures.

At first the honeymoon, then the slow grinding down and
numbing domesticity, the usual progression of conjugal love.
Followed by boredom and lies. That was the modern way,
hardly anyone she knew lived differently. Her parents, perhaps,
but who knew finally the true lives of their parents?

Though often that did not count either: Some couples
seemed content together but hated each other; some fought
viciously before friends and children but were more in love

than when they first met. Odd how the ones who stayed in love did not notice—or seem to mind too much—how each grew older, seeing each other always at the age they had met and were always on fire, though the heat had long ago cooled down. Would that happen to her and to Rex?

But they had not, or had not as yet, gone tepid. They seldom quarreled or complained to one another. If ever, it was she who initiated the complaint, urging him to work less, to eat more—he seemed almost too skinny—to take more time—not for her, but for himself. To do what? he asked, when all that he did he did for himself, since she and the boy and he were all the same self.

She had become a little bourgeois wife, Rex said. Perhaps, maybe there was something to bourgeois life after all? Who thought they would ever come to this, the two of them, planning meals and outings with the boy, keeping house, doing laundry; the everyday matters that ordinarily dull the spirit and sex by sameness.

Better nothing than the same fare served up on the same plate; better hunger, for that still meant sensation. But he still had the power, even in her imagination, to arouse her, to make her feel that her deepest life had its center in his voice, in the semidarkness, as he called her to bed.

She had started to write again. Back to Poussin, an artist who made even Cézanne seem fiery. Here she was in the heat of love, and also in love with a child who was as much her own as if she had given birth to him—her life a springtime pond, ripe with twirling spirogyra and splitting amoebae, bulging with tadpoles and ducklings, a living warm broth—but something in her wished for a place more glacial. For some geometry of perfection, of irreducible and immutable forms struck from the surface of thought, the forms that Plato had so long ago divined and, she imagined, Poussin had at times translated into his art.

How much time had passed when one day she returned home from the *bibliothèque*, where she spent mornings writing, to find an envelope leaning against a vase with one rose? She smelled a death sentence. His timing would be perfect, to leave her now—and once again—when she was and they were happy, the happiest they had ever been or could ever be.

"Dominique," the letter began. "When I came to Paris, I was looking for barricades and walls of paving stones blocking the avenues; I thought the revolution was hours away and that I would be part of it. I left New York and you because I needed to do this for myself, maybe for the gamble of it, my life with you or the revolution.

"My life with you seemed to hold no future; it was your life I would be living. After all, what was to become of me in a place where I didn't fit and didn't want to fit? Your studies and the life it promised afterward, the life in fact that you were having when we recently met in Paris, did not channel with mine or rightly or wrongly with my way of thinking. You are at heart a bourgeois aesthete.

"Of course, we lost the revolution (that word seems so strange and archaic now, like 'milkman' or 'wax paper' or 'ice box') in Paris a decade and more earlier. Maybe the revolution should have been lost. But what hopeful idea has replaced it? But that's another story.

"There were a lot of foreigners like myself still hanging around Paris who had dreamed the same '68 dream. I met this woman—she was nothing like Olga, who was all talk and who had lived a nice life with the other middle-class Mexican radicals; all those artists and intellectuals in cozy setups, going to caviar receptions at the Soviet Embassy.

"Tamara was born very rich, perhaps had even more wealth than she let on. She made no secret of it, actually. She said that when the time came she'd return to Tokyo and kill her parents personally and not in their sleep, either.

"She had received the best education and spoke French and English perfectly, frighteningly so. That Japanese face making all those perfect Western sounds—and Spanish, too, I almost forgot.

"She had been to Cuba and most of South America and had gone underground with several of the groups there before coming to Paris. She thought like a guerrilla, a spy, a hunted revolutionary. She carried no address book, all her phone numbers were memorized, just in case she was arrested and tortured, as she had been in South America. She carried a few passports, fake ones, and she had no bank account or credit cards or anything that could trace her, really identify her. To this day I still do not know her real name.

"She did not fit well in Paris. She hated the French CP because she believed they were the same as the Soviets: bourgeois and reactionary. The only thing that had stood between France and the revolution in '68, she said, had been the French Communist Party. She was still pissed off with the Party after all these years. She didn't like the rest of the Left either, maybe with the exception of the old Maoists, but she thought they were bullshit, too, with their little Red Books and Marxist mantras. She did believe in much of Maoism and in parts of the Red Book, she just didn't think it would work in the industrial West, where there were no mountains and remote areas for the revolutionary guerrilla to disappear, like fish into the vast sea of the masses.

"I'm sure you remember Kyo, the Japanese revolutionary in Malraux's *Man's Fate*. Kyo was her ideal. Dedicated and disciplined and visionary and ready to die, to be boiled alive, if need be (as Kyo finally was), for the hope of human freedom. I liked Tamara for her idealism, for her devotion to that time far away when the world would be finally set right, without private property, without privilege or status or hierarchy of any sort.

"In a way she was the story of the old Left, maybe closer to the spirit of the Nihilists and Anarchists of the Russia of the 1880s than to anything in our time. Did you ever read Andreyev's *The Seven Who Were Hanged*, about comrades about to be executed, triumphant in their complicity and in their martyrdom, as are all true believers? Those types have the best of everything. She thought so, in any case.

"When we went to a café she paid with a thick wad of francs stuffed in her jeans. Sometimes bills would just fall on the table, on the floor, five-hundred-, thousand-franc notes, the waiter would just stare at all those crumpled bills and then at us, two misfits with all that cash.

"She had an upper-floor apartment on the Ile St. Louis facing the Seine, with the best stereo equipment housed in a custom-made teakwood cabinet, where she kept more stacks of serious cash; she tooled around Paris on a Harley-Davidson and had her leathers made in Florence, very supple, creamy black. For all her wealth and the cushy way she lived, she felt *I* was not quite OK, that I was just another bourgeois guy not to be trusted, and finally, not to like. I was very impure in her eyes, as was everyone, unless he had died for the revolution.

"She liked her cat, Nicolino, and wrestled on the carpet with him, her little panther. She fed him caviar from Petrossian once or twice a week; leaving little pots of unpressed beluga in the middle of the living room for him to consider. She had no lovers that I knew. But who knows?

"She once bought me a carton of Gauloise yellow and took me to Maxim's once to lunch—the front room—just to show me how deliciously one could live, born the right way. All acquired wealth she considered theft, and the born-to-it kind just inherited theft. She was a child of thieves, she said, as were all the children of the rich. At least that leaves us out, Dominique. Finally, she was a child of her class with all their spoiled ways, but could not see herself as such.

"I did not love her. I have not loved anyone since you. You are always inside me blocking anyone else from entering too deeply. But I liked her, even with her contradictions and her arrogance; maybe I liked her because she showed no interest in sleeping with me. 'What do you do for sex?' I asked her once.

'I shoot pricks like you,' she answered. 'In the balls, first.'

"She had a little Beretta to prove it and waved it under my nose in the Buttes-Chaumont one afternoon. In that grotto with the cascading waterfalls, she just pulled that piece out and made me smell it. She thought it very funny that I complained about her waving a pistol around in public, showing that my fear proved how conventional a man I was. A normal man, that's all, I was just another normal man, she said, with pretensions to being something else.

"I was sure she would shoot me, I told her, because killing was preferable to admitting that she was afraid of sex and—even worse—to revealing she was a corpse in bed. That stung her, all rebuff did.

"I let her stew and didn't call or see her for a few days. She wasn't afraid of sex or of anything else in this world, she explained on the phone a week later, calling me at four in the morning. As for bed, she was better than anything I had ever experienced in my bourgeois life with lifeless bourgeois girls.

"I started to laugh but she wasn't joking: Once, in the early seventies, she had brought a man back to life after he had been tortured in an Argentine prison for months, a man without will to live, broken, jelly with a human shell, this comrade, and she got him so hot he forgot prison and the electric shocks on his balls and dreamed only of fucking her day and night. Imagine then how she could benefit a normal man, she said, if only she wanted to. That made me howl, Dominique, the 'benefit.' Of course she took it badly, my laughing like that, and she said that the next time she saw me she'd shoot a bullet up my ass.

"'The balls, the ass,' I said. 'Don't you ever go for a clean heart shot, or one through the head?'

"She came over an hour later at five just as I was falling back to sleep. I was so tired and she was so inert that I'm still not sure whether I really fucked her or not. She undressed in the dark and wouldn't let me see her naked in bed, and once in a while she twitched like a flounder dying on a cutting board. No sooner than it was over—and that was very soon—she got dressed again and split. She turned to me at the door and with a look of great self-satisfaction and triumph said, 'So there.' And as an afterthought she added, 'Goodbye, asshole.'

"That was it for a while. I didn't even run into her at the

usual haunts. And after some months I was sure she had left Paris, that she had gotten bored with the revolution, with Paris, and had returned home. Lenin was suspicious of intellectual revolutionaries and of those from the rich—while they still had their money.

"All their good intentions and struggles for justice were just episodes of play, while the real show was waiting for them at home, with Mom and Dad, with the wonderful ease and safety they were born to. Would you desire a revolution if you had a live-in cook? At the end of everything, only true killers see the revolution thing through, like Lenin.

"Would you believe how little all that matters to me now? I am no different from all those I criticized, now that only you and Kenji make up my world.

"Then she called me one day to invite me to dinner, very cheerful, almost friendly. A fancy place in the Palais Royale gardens, where the history of Paris had dined. It's an experience to eat like that at least once in your life. I had the lamb rack with baby roast potatoes and rosemary. I can still taste the lamb.

"She didn't eat much because she was always throwing up, she said, from being pregnant. It was mine, of course. From that enlivening night nine months earlier. She was ready to drop any hour; you wouldn't know it though; from the way she looked she was carrying nothing larger than a grapefruit.

"A little ball with red hair, that Kenji boy. She delivered him on her apartment floor, on a mat, because that was the way Andean peasants gave birth, on the earthen floor of their mountain huts. She didn't want her nipples bitten, she said, so she found a wet nurse through an agency and let the young woman suckle Kenji for the first six months.

"I was useless, actually. I did all the crappy work of changing diapers and wiping his sweet little ass and generally acting as his cleanup man; I did the things I could. She had a horror of the whole matter, a genuine physical recoil in his presence; the noise, the waking up and crying at all hours, the helplessness of this little mess of desires made her weak and frightened. She withdrew and she shriveled. Sometimes I thought she was dead, lying there in the center of her bed, her arms crossed, eyes shut, silent and frozen to me, to her son, to the room.

"Six months ago she split and left him with me. Then, a few weeks later, she left us both. She would not be trapped in the walls of a bourgeois life, she said. I could do what I pleased, keep him or put him up for adoption. Why hadn't she had an abortion, I wanted to know? Because it would bring her bad luck, she said; it would haunt her, the mangled ghost of that embryo following her everywhere she went.

"She gave up her flat and left Paris. I have no idea where she went, where she is, or what she is doing. Of course, the boy regards every woman as his mother, and he's right insofar as women love him. You most of all are his 'Mum ma.'"

The paragraph broke abruptly, as if Rex had gotten to the end of what he felt he had to tell to clear the slate with her or as if all that he had said was the foundation for the exhortation that followed:

"My darling," it began, "let's be regular, have an ordinary life. Let's not try to be special or do exceptional things. Men and women have tried to figure out how to find harmony and maybe even some pleasure with each other. So few have. Let's not be like them. Let's go for something rare. Let's give to each other what devotion we once thought to give to the revolution."

She read the letter three times and put it in her suitcase, still standing, from the time she moved in, half empty in the hallway. She brought Kenji up to their neighbors, leaving him bundled against the chilling fall dampness, against the gray walls and grayer dome of the suburb with streets named after dead poets and Resistance fighters, bundled against everything icy from the past and present that would chill the child's soul.

He had looked at her with eyes very wise and old, like an ancient Japanese woodcutter in a magical forest suspended in mountain mists, and followed her to the door, letting her leave without a reproach or protest.

"Go wing," he said, and then, "Mum ma."

And then she left, missing him even more than if he had tried to stay her leaving. She wanted to turn back and sweep him up and take him with her, but Rex's pull was stronger and she rushed down the stairs.

# CHAPTER 15

SHE TURNED DOWN to the square named after Robert Desnos, the surrealist poet, who died in a Nazi death camp, and came to the shop—open to the street—where Rex repaired and built bicycles, where he tested out his dreams. He was out for a break—*une pause*—Alain, the owner, said, giving her a casual once-over from habit, she was sure; his eyes acting on their own, seeing through her jacket and blouse and bra right to her naked breasts. She didn't mind, today. With Rex's letter in her suitcase she was invulnerable, even to Superman's X-ray vision.

"Alain," she said, familiarly—he had called her Dominique on their first introduction, with a casualness she felt was close to insolence, alternating her name with a few "mademoiselles" to let her know he did not regard her as married to Rex, a courtesy he perhaps might have given her had she been French. Although, finally, she was not certain that he was disrespectful at all but trying in his own way to behave with the casualness of the Americans he had seen in the movies.

"Alain, why don't you sell Rex your business or at least make him your partner?"

He smiled and offered her a cigarette. "And why is it that Rex does not ask me this?"

He blew a perfect smoke ring above her head, and then another. There was that place in New York long ago where Rex's smoke rings bounced along the walls and rolled across the floor, taking over the room, and then all the rooms, until she thought to leave and go where they could not follow.

"Alain," she said, "it would be so good for you to do that, to let Rex build the wonderful bikes he wants so that the two of you may become wealthy and renowned."

He studied her. What could he learn from her face that he did not from her words? She had learned from his expression that he was sincerely puzzled, that his raised eyebrows made him look more startled than interested by what she had said.

"I'm not too much for the glory, mademoiselle," he said finally, with a certain weariness. And dignity, she thought. A mechanic in a Léger painting, wrench in hand, blue coveralls hanging like a wide bag of breeze.

She found Rex at the bar of a nearby café speaking intently with two men from his shop; he was explaining to them how some spokes made from titanium would lighten the wheel frame by a significant fraction, and from there he turned to considering the weight of the bike itself—though it seemed they had heard him on that part before and were now returning to their drinks.

He looked the happiest she had known him. So at ease with himself and free of all the world but the one in which he was now living. He saw her, smiled and beckoned her over. The others received her politely but rather shyly, she thought. She had invaded their enclave, bringing unwelcome vistas from the world of four wheels and strollers. For a moment she thought how it must have struck them as unusual for a wife to enter their domain, so to speak, in the afternoon, and she saw in Rex's face a moment of alarm.

"No, nothing is wrong," she said.

She just felt the need to see him. To kiss his face and eyes, she wanted to say, to tell him that his letter had enfolded her and had removed any vestige of bitter memories of their past, when they were so careless with each other, with their sense of youth's eternity of time. But she would wait until he came home—having now seen him. She knew he understood.

They laughed, and she walked home stronger in her conviction of their tie and now resolved to bring her plan to life.

"Alain, why don't you sell Rex your business, or at least make him your partner?" she had asked. Impromptu, impulsive, an idea inhabiting no zone of her thoughts before that instant. Yet when she said it she knew it was what she wanted, to have Rex realize his dream, to have him move up and ahead, on his own terms, as Americans were supposed to do. But that reality seemed far away. Rex could not afford to buy a bike from the shop he worked in, let alone buy the shop itself, or half of it.

She sat in the café beneath their apartment and smoked three cigarettes in succession and sent her heart to further effort with two strong espressos. That morning she had seen a mouse run across the floor where Kenji slept. Where there was one, there were surely others, and perhaps worse. Ali told her there were no rats where there were mice, but she was not convinced.

She had admonished Kenji not to bring food to his bed—his mattress on the floor—because it attracted mice. He took the slice of bread he had been eating and shredded it, scattering the crumbs over the floor. He looked at her, smiling.

"Mices, come, come mices, come, come," he said gleefully.

They were small and not dangerous creatures, but they were vermin and not sweet little Mickeys and Minnies. Though she had kept the apartment clean, scrubbed, the windows bright, every surface sparkling, the sour undercoat of a make-do life was waiting to rise. Kenji took the mice as friends, like the sparrows, like the butterflies in the park, like everything in his wonderful world.

Soon her university money would run out, and while her book on Poussin would one day appear, there was no money to come from that, or from any other book she might publish in the future. There was no money to expect from her family, who were hinting at difficulties in their letters; their hints were another's storm warnings. "We've sprung a leak." Meaning that their hull was staved in and sucking up the Atlantic.

They could return to America and she could take up her life again. She had been writing as much in Paris as she ever would in New York; the salary she would receive on her return to teaching being the only—and significant—difference.

But why would Rex want to leave, now that he had found his life revolving about two wheels on a frame? And, finally, did she want to leave the streets of dead poets and the beautiful gray skies and the cold branches and the green light of their apartment?

She wrote Eric a short note, unsentimental and without flirtation. She made no bribe of emotion, offered no hint of present or future personal reward should he favor her request. She wanted him to consider her request only and not herself. It was a dry, almost curt note, and so without flavor or enticement as to suggest to her that she almost wished him to refuse her.

Of course, she also knew that such a starched note was ultimately directed to the fullness of his feelings for her and that it was his feelings that would dictate his decision and not the business side of her proposal. She told herself that in light of the impersonality of her words, she was not responsible should he attach some other meaning or hope to them and thus she could believe that she was not exploiting him, but she could not fully convince herself of that.

At the end of two weeks, she had not heard from him. She was slightly relieved but more than surprised that her meaning to him had diminished so completely, and in some unexpected way, her estimation of him rose.

At the start of the third week he phoned; he happened to be in Paris on business. She was sure he was lying. She liked that he had lied and kept his dignity. When they met he said right off that she was the business he had come for, thus exploding his cover, but his confession was delivered in such a perfunctory and casual way as to suggest that it was just something polite and charming to say.

In terms of his worldly presentation, he was better dressed than when she met him a little more than a year earlier—even his shoes were Italian and handmade. They kissed on the cheeks, two old friends. He had taken the same suite at the Ritz they had shared a lifetime ago, but now he sat more comfortably in the Louis Quatorze replica and showed kingly disregard for the pages squeezing out from the fax machine behind him.

"You look quite distinguished," she said.

Even now she could not resist the banter, the ironic edge which concealed, but barely, her disrespect for everything in him she was—as she painfully admitted to herself—attracted to.

He smiled but did not engage her and brought the subject to her work, which during their separation he had read, all her essays and articles and even her doctoral thesis on Goya's cartoons for tapestries. He was waiting for her to finish her Poussin book; he was interested in what she would say, especially now that he had had the chance to see the paintings in whatever city he found himself on business. She smiled appreciatively.

Had he gotten richer since they last walked together? she asked. Wanting to take the subject of herself off the table, or from any platform suggesting horizontality. Not vastly, he answered, but considerably—just money with legs, running ahead of his thoughts.

Himself, he said—returning to his theme—he found Poussin dreary, could not imagine why she had pursued him or given him more of her time than it took to glance over the pictures in a gallery. Everything in Poussin was so correct and frozen, he said, without a hint, she felt, of trying to provoke or irritate her. His dismissal of the artist she had spent years in thinking and writing about might be understood as his questioning of her sensibility—all that work, for what?

"That's all right," she said. "I wonder the same myself sometimes."

She did not mean it too seriously; but she could not make the effort to tell him that at times all she had written faded into memory, leaving behind in her mind an image representing all of Poussin's work: an equilateral triangle imbedded in a cave of dark trees, bathed in light neither day nor night, dawn nor dusk, but from the well of all light, varnished and glowing in golden black, in Old Master fashion. All Poussin's allegories and narratives, sheep, shepherds, nymphs, gods sleeping in bowers, all were obliterated and transformed into a triangle partnered to an impossible light.

Eric was comfortable with himself, his shirt open at the neck, sitting casually in a suite the weekly cost of half a year of her old salary, excluding tax—but his ease did not come from his money, since he was fidgety with her only a few hundred million dollars and a year ago. She sensed also that his assurance had nothing to do with their present situation or with his power to help her. She did not feel she had lent him that power or had lowered herself a fraction to a supplicant's stoop. He could have said, or made her feel: Nice of you to contact me when you're in need. But there was none of that.

"Well," he said, in a friendly manner, "I suppose you just want to get to it."

"It's not all business, Eric," she said, not wishing to seem rude, to seem impatient, not to seem, finally, interested only in the matter she had come for.

But he overrode her politeness and went to the heart of her letter, saying that in principle he would help her, although he did not quite understand the specifics of her proposal. Whatever it was, however, he had already found a French lawyer to deal with what had to be done.

When she told him exactly what she wanted and its exact purpose, he did not flinch. He bettered her by suggesting that if the current owner did not want to enter into a partnership or sell his business to Rex, he would simply set Rex up on his own. Eventually, he'd take a share of the profits, which, considering the nature of the operation, would never amount to much—not real money—but he liked the idea of bikes in general and of handcrafted ones in particular.

Not much money and not much passion for the ambition itself, so why would he make the effort to put any time or money into the project? she asked.

He gave her a long and, she thought, studied look. Perhaps one he used in his business negotiations to unsteady his adversaries, to keep them guessing. It worked on her. Whatever he had in mind she would never know, because he quickly shifted expression and with it the tense atmosphere.

"Well, I'd expect a decent return. And decent discount on a bike for myself—don't you think that's fair?" he added, smiling in a way that relaxed her. "But we don't need a contract for all that, just a handshake."

"Just a handshake," she repeated.

Outside his window, on the Place Vendôme, Napoleon's prize from the Egyptian campaign once stood. A column pulled down during the early days of the Paris Commune by insurgents eager to destroy monuments of the old order. Implicated in the destruction, Courbet was arrested after the Commune was suppressed; he was nearly deported to the tropical Guiana, along with the thousands of others who were sent there to repent in the heat.

She did not like Courbet's paintings overmuch, but he had kept himself on the radical path all his life—the road menders and the peasants of his paintings walked beside him on that path of humane intentions. Courbet had painted them—bent at their outdoor work, boys and girls thickened by the sun, at ten looking twenty. He showed the working world in its dignity and patience.

Yet, finally, perhaps he did not love that world deeply enough, because it was his paintings not of workers but of bourgeois young women sitting on a swatch of rich green grass by a flowing narrow brook that showed his real love. Showed his attraction to a world where women's creamy white arms and soft hands denoted protection beyond that of parasols and white gloves, showed his affinity for a bourgeois calm and ease, grace and courtesy—the class rights of its privileged members: every luscious brushstroke spoke for that love in him.

She was about to tell Eric about the piece of history out his window but she remembered the last time she had played his guide, when they were still on the eve of their affair and he found her charming—or pretended he did—even at her most didactic. It would not be so charming now, her exposition on the iconoclasm of the first Communist revolution, when she was on the verge, so to speak, of entering into her first capitalist alliance.

"Well, one day I hope you'll come and meet Rex and the boy," she said, after a long pause.

"I doubt it," he answered neutrally. "It's not in my province."

It was done. There was really no more to add now, unless it was on the personal terrain, but for now, at least, he clearly did not want to venture there. She felt like an employee who had delivered her report and was now expected to exit the boss's office smoothly and without too much fuss.

She extended her hand.

"A shake then," she said. He took her hand, pressing it not too hard, not too softly, not personally but not impersonally, familiarly and firmly enough but without pushing the boundary to that land of the extra, to the remember-my-words-to-you-at-the-bridge, and the I-still-want-you territory. Maybe, in fact, he no longer wanted her; that was possible, but she did not believe it, letting the thought depart as quickly as it had appeared.

She left, returning home and to the café below her window, and ordered a marc, then nursed two more. The Muslims at their tables sipping mint tea did not approve of women drinking, especially a mother, especially Rex's wife; they did not approve of it anyway for anyone. She did not approve of herself for the moment. Not for asking for and taking the money—that would be in the world of its own dynamic and bring with it its own concerns, as did all money and what was done with it—but for being drawn to Eric's aplomb and newly acquired sense of power, for being attracted to his keeping on his side of the fence. Even though she did not want him to cross over it, she had wanted him to show that he wished to.

Now she was being sententious, one drink more and she'd be moralizing. But Rex, detaching himself from a trio of colleagues from his shop, came to rescue her.

"Now, darling," he said, amused by her wide grin and tipsy sway, "you seem to be partying all by yourself. Where's the fun in that?"

"I'm in the province of one," she said.

"Any visitors allowed in?"

"May . . . be. Try applying for a visa."

"What's the fee for one these days?" he asked.

"It was three marcs five minutes ago but it's just gone up to four. Can you manage that?"

Rex casually downed the three marcs he ordered and had set in a row, leaving the fourth on guard between them.

"Leave it there," she said, "and let's finish the party at home."

Soon they were in bed, the world's clock set at zero.

"Are we still young?" she asked, feeling as if they were still in Montauk, immortal and fresh, like the frisky sea.

"Close enough, anyway," he answered. "And that's how we'll stay."

"Wait," she said, as he was dressing to retrieve the boy she was once again longing to hold. "Wait till you hear the news I've brought you."

# CHAPTER 16

"WISDOM," PROFESSOR MORIN answered. He was perhaps fifty, but to Dominique, in her early twenties, he had emerged from the previous century. Not everyone his age had seemed so antique, so far from the modern world, though he was, at least superficially, current and rarely judgmental of contemporary culture and its art, which even at her age she found mostly the apotheosis of mediocrity.

His manners, his courtesy, his mind identified him as the old European, polished but not slippery and with just enough uneven touches—like the small egg spots on the lapels of his pin-striped suit—to make him seem endearingly flawed. His only other suit, the same, but a shade more charcoal than its double, was equally spotted and stained. Those egg splotches the equivalent of the rhetorician's affected stutter, the slight flaw impeding the otherwise too smooth flow of words, and thus proving the speaker's sincerity and artlessness.

"What is it you treasure most, Samuel, the thing you most wish to have?" Dominique asked after lunch, when he had come to visit her on his way through Madrid that fall years ago, when she was putting the finishing touches to her dissertation.

"Wisdom," he answered. "All else follows from it, especially compassion."

That was a lovely reply but she was not sure whether, in fact, it wasn't the wise thing a professor of his generation was expected to believe—or say—along with the old-fashioned idea that knowledge of Latin was required for a classical education. All those notions were so ancient, like so much dust settled on the coffin floor, after corpse and bones had vanished in the wash of time. Still memorable, all that dust.

"What's wrong with serenity?" she said. "I'd rather own that than wisdom."

"Serenity follows from wisdom," he answered. "There's no serenity without it."

What of a serenity born of resignation, she thought, the serenity of just giving up—of folding your cards, as Rex might have said and leaving the game for others to play?

She could have argued around the Professor's idea for another half hour or half a year. But she left off, because he was, for all their friendship and supposed equality, her professor and mentor and thus her superior. Also because she wanted to credit or "privilege"—as her younger colleagues were currently saying—his hierarchy of virtues, as much for herself as for him.

He was among the last ribbons tied to the humanist tradition, with its assumed canons and golden values. Values she once—and to some degree still—considered the lies of class and privilege, but which appealed to her ever more strongly as she grew older. The life of the mind, as it was once termed, was for her, if not the life of serenity, then the life of decency, and perhaps even of goodness.

What was the wisdom of what she had done for Rex, and what serenity had evolved from her action? Rex, the bike designer and builder, was—for want of a more exact word—more serene than she had ever known him to be. He was no longer the man who had brooded on Keats and who had once plunged himself into ocean and revolution. It was the wisdom of her action, she was sure, that had led him—and her—to this greater happiness, this serenity.

The orders came in, his old clients betting on Rex's ability to make them merge with their machines and fly on bikes fitted to their weight and height and posture. Each bike tailored to its owner, like a custom suit. The first bike to leave the shop was made for a cyclist who had never placed better than third in the competitions.

"I am locked into third," he said to Rex when he came for the fitting. "I do not even dream of first," he added, "but carry me to second, Monsieur Rex, and I shall be grateful."

He was a small man, wiry and disappointed by the road. Monsieur Fischer, a French Swiss with a small chateau packed with bikes. He offered to double the bike's price should he win the next race, but when he saw the machine with its baked red enamel frame, dull tires, and shiny gears, he declared his offer ignoble—the bribe of a tradesman. He would give Rex double the amount no matter where he placed in the race—purely for the emotion the bicycle gave him, like the delicate shiver of falling in love. Rex prized the sentiment but rejected his generous offer.

"Don't be silly," Dominique said. "He has enough money to make the gesture and it suits him to make it."

She said that, but in truth she thought Rex gallant, liking him the more for being so; for some—for her—gallantry being more a magnet for love than money. In the end, Monsieur Fischer barely placed fourth but it was not the machine's fault, he said in a note to Rex, for it had performed impeccably, unlike its owner, who at forty was simply beyond his time to compete in such races.

Rex's reputation was increasing and there was a waiting list within the first year. He did not need many clients, some two dozen would keep his operation stable and the quality of the work high, by his standards. He would never grow rich but he would flourish. They would flourish.

"Wisdom" Professor Morin had treasured above all, but he might have added "bounty"—wisdom's bed.

When Kenji was five, they moved from St. Denis to a two-bedroom flat overlooking the Parc Monceau. It would have cost a fortune to rent but the building's owner and the proprietor of several other buildings deluxe valued money less than a beautiful bike—there were such capitalist anomalies, Dominique had learned, although she believed they were rare.

From her wide window she could see Kenji in a line with other children from his school as they were being taken to the playground. He was holding the hand of a little girl he loved, Olivia, and speaking to her with great emphasis. Then he kissed her. And they both laughed. He turned away from her and waved his free hand to the sky.

She was writing one of her fragments, a paragraph on the fascist murder of the poet Garcia Lorca, but seeing Kenji in his blue coveralls and open red sandals and blue peaked cap, seeing him in his excitement, had distracted her. He was usually reserved, even with her and Rex. Solemn, someone once said, without being moody. He stayed apart, studying the pictures in a book or working out a puzzle by himself, even when with those his age, except when with Olivia.

"Do you like Olivia?" she asked one day.

"Yes, I do, Mama."

"More than the other girls in your class?"

"Yes."

"More than Danielle?"

She had been the favorite for a long time, all through the previous winter and spring. He had made drawings for her of horses riding the ocean waves. He read to her from his favorite books, making up the stories as he went along, since he could not yet read.

"Danielle," he said, "is at the window."

"And Olivia?"

"She is at the center of the room, Mama."

He had his own little room now. With a door and a window overlooking a courtyard garden in bloom throughout the spring. She had a place to read and work and withdraw, to drift away with the trees and the life of the beautiful park.

Rex built her a ledge by the window where she could curl up and dream. She read her mother's letter at that ledge.

It finally had happened. Through manpower shortages, through the competition of larger and more efficient boats owned by fishing corporations—some foreign—through her aging father's inability to sustain the long stays at sea, through time and human entropy, her father, taking loans against their home, had lost the boat and was forced to sell the house.

They were moving up island, where life was cheaper. Where, Dominique thought, they knew no one, where there was no ocean beneath their window, where they, even with all their customary goodwill and bravery, their uncomplaining-ness, would soon rot. Malls, parking fields, the multiplex with the summer hit movies all year long, the video shops and their colorized classics, the gas stations and their democracy of self-service, the pizza shacks with pies of 101 toppings, including pineapple: They were voyaging up island to the dead, dead middle.

She would not permit a European to say the dismal things she thought about her country, but she knew America was lev-eling, its spiritual beauty vanishing along with the beautiful land.

The height of folly, the Greeks thought, was to beat the sea with chains. As she was now doing, in her grief and anger. Was she the only angry one? Many Americans were in the same plight as her parents and worse; they did not seem to protest. When she was in France she could see America dispassion-ately, she thought.

"That's the free market," Rex said, after she told him what had happened. "It's only as good as it works for you."

"What a great consoler you are," she said with ironic cheer.

He put his arm around her shoulder. "Of course, I'm sorry, for your parents," he said.

"What's happening to America?" she asked, raising her head to him. "What's changed?"

"Oh!" Rex said. "Except for the very top, it's turning into the Third World."

"The Third World." She laughed. "No one calls it the Third World anymore."

"Just because you change the words, Dominique, doesn't mean you've changed the conditions."

She saw beside her the passionate young man in college who read Marx and Engels with the same concentration and belief he gave to the mystic teachings of Don Juan, who could turn himself into a crow and fly over deserts. What did she believe?

They were walking through the park on the way to pick up Kenji from school. The windows of their apartment mirrored clouds drifting to nowhere but dissolution; the world moved with their drift and slow tumble: how much like the billows of dreams floated up by dreamy youth. Her youth.

The clouds in Poussin's paintings were unreal, like plaster fixtures stuck in the sky; his narratives, unlike Goya's, were bloodless and cerebral, however much she tried to squeeze from them the dramas of human life. Posssin's formal conceptions were powerful to her, speaking for a transcendental but not earthy reality, the buildings, pillars, steps in his canvases having the same emotional weight as his human figures, which finally were just shapes and forms in the painting's composition.

Her interest in him, when she felt such emotional remove from his art and such doubt about what she was writing, mystified her. Not what she was writing, but why she was doing it at all. Perhaps there were deep secrets in his art, but she was not sure she had the analytical temperament to uncover them.

Her father had taken her to the Metropolitan Museum when she was nine. He was struck, he told her when she was older, by how she had concentrated on a Poussin painting. She did not like his paintings in the museum as much as the one she had loved in her book, where shepherds and a woman stood before a mysterious tomb. The picture high on the museum wall made her feel dizzy. Not from the figures mounting and descending the marble steps on their way to and from an open temple housing the miracle of St. Peter and St. John healing a lame man, and not by the miracle itself, but because of the shapes abstracted from the human figures, the thick heft of the temple columns and the squarish blocks of buildings massed behind them. They spoke to her of a life out of nature, pure and enduring.

"More than any other painter of the seventeenth century?" Professor Morin had once asked.

"More than anyone else and as much as Cézanne and Picasso," she answered without pausing to think. She did not need to, having thought it out long ago, before she was born, or else how to explain her pull to Poussin when she was a young girl, recognizing herself among all those stiff columns and stiffer figures in the Poussin painting her father had brought her to see.

"Isn't there anything we can do for them, Rex?" she asked.

"They seem to have done it all already, Dominique."

It was not reassuring, what he said, not comforting, as even a lie might comfort.

With all their goodwill, there was nothing she or Rex could do or could have done for them. Only money had the power to change her parents' lives, and she never would have enough of that. Her lofty ideas had taken her where she could live among a painting's pillars and columns, in a temple where miracles happened, but they could not pay the mortgage on the house or caulk a sinking boat.

# CHAPTER 17

THEY WERE WALKING through the park on the way to pick up Kenji from school, where he would be waiting, book in hand, on a bench in the quiet entrance hall. Waiting, looking at the pictures and telling himself stories. When she came alone, he would feel her at the door watching him. *"Maman est arrivée,"* he would say to the book, and slide off the bench, hug her, kiss her hand and hold it all the way back home.

They walked, hand in hand. Rex's still soiled from work. The chestnut trees lining the street glowed in the afternoon sun; the café, where they would stop on their way home, sent out its chatter of plates and aroma of coffee and wine, as it did yesterday and the day before and would tomorrow.

This day that was so perfect would give birth to a perfect future, where she would grow old and Rex would never notice her aging, and where he would grow old and she would see him as young as he was on this day. Their beautiful world would never end so long as they were alive—and they would always be alive. Death would never penetrate their Arcadia.

In a line that stayed with her long after she had forgotten much else but his call for self-reliance, Emerson said: "Once you have plumbed the depths of a man, that's the end of him." What else is there, after all, to keep one interested except the continual letting out of the endless line into the seemingly fathomless depth of a person? A depth of her own invention, she might concede to herself in a ruthless, honest moment, imagining depths in Rex when there was only his disappearances, his frightening unpredictability.

He had been thinking, Rex said after a long silence, of giving up the bike business. She was taken aback but said nothing, waiting for the rest.

"It's the owning part that I don't like," he said, "and having people working for me."

She reminded him that he long ago had set up a profit-sharing plan for the employees and that, in fact, the operation was run more like a commune than a business. He was the creative brains as well as an artisan among several—and where was the wrong in that? He wasn't sitting in some faraway office and collecting the rewards of his investment. Yes, that was true, he conceded her that. It helped him to be reminded. It was just a thought, in any case, he added. Just a little thought.

"I'm not reassured," she said; not in their three and a half years of living together had she ever been, she wanted to add.

"Isn't it I who should feel reassured?" he asked.

What a strange word, to assure again, to re-assure. With Rex, once the notion seized him, any word could mean whatever he wanted.

"Well, in the sense that you are assuring again your own decision not to leave the business, of course. But I'm not convinced that you won't do that, now that it's in your head."

He laughed. "You sure have complicated ways of saying things, and you say them without having to write them out first."

"Where would we go and what would we do? Have you thought that far ahead?"

No, of course not. She could sense that. Like his plunge into the ocean; it was the plunge that mattered, not what came afterward.

"Are you going to drown us all?" she continued.

"What a strange jump of thought, Red," he said. He turned and took her in his arms and kissed her in the old reassuring way he had whenever she was worried. The eyes first and then the lips.

When they arrived at the school, the hallway was empty and the bench vacant. Madame Ledoux, the school's administrator, was still in her office, as were two children waiting to be taken home. But neither child was Kenji. Madame seemed pleased but surprised to see them, and after Dominique greeted her and asked where Kenji was, Madame let out a little shriek of fear.

"But madame," she said, "his uncle came to take him home, as you had requested in your note."

# CHAPTER 18

EVEN YEARS LATER, walking alone thinking of this or that, a bill yet to be paid or what she would write in a review or how she would position a shrub beside a rock in a garden bounded by a cliff dropping over the ocean, she felt the same pain of that first moment in the hallway when she understood that Kenji was gone.

At first they believed, along with the police, that it was a kidnapping, but after a week of silence, they prayed it was a kidnapping—with its attendant promise to see Kenji again. But when no ransom was ever demanded and no contact was ever made, they feared he had been picked up by a pedophile—or else why no ransom request? The ploy had been too elaborately staged for that, the police said. Molesters of children waited in parks or outside school buildings to make their snatches. The ruse of the Japanese uncle was too calculated, too professional, for an amateur operation.

She saw him forever as she had last, when, in a crush of others at the school entrance, he turned, giving her a long tender look, his brow knitted as if reading, and waved and said, "Kiss you, Mama."

It was Rex who first understood. The Japanese uncle and the letter written surprisingly, as Madame had said, in excellent French. That should have made her suspicious, Madame said, the excellence of the note's style, but seeing that he was a Japanese man gave her confidence, she said, Kenji being one of their kind. She had even taken the precaution of telephoning Dominique, but as she did not answer, she felt further proof of the legitimacy of the uncle and the letter.

It was the boy's mother or her family that had taken him, Rex said one afternoon as they left the police station, where they had become regulars, eliciting the sympathy of the most hardened detectives and even those at Interpol who had given the matter their attention. Kenji's face appeared on posters and on TV in six countries, with the expression, caught by Rex's camera, of a slightly parted mouth and widened eyes, of wonder as an elephant raised his trunk to him through the bars of the zoo.

Not that Rex's theory had any way helped to find the boy. Even after he acted on his suspicions by confiding them to the authorities, Rex realized he did not know the family name of Kenji's mother or where she had come from in Japan or, as he had once told Dominique, much of anything about her. With such vagueness, what could they do, the police said.

"The rich," noted one inspector, seemingly given to aphorism, "can do much of what they want. And the very rich can do all of what they want."

And, then, there was too the matter of legality: Even if Rex's theory was correct, did not the mother, were she ever found, have a right to her child, and would Rex not have to dispute that right in the Japanese courts? A process that might take years, assuming he had the money to cover the legal costs.

Dominique took some consolation in Rex's theory. At least Kenji was not dead or victimized, as she vaguely put it, fearful of conjuring up the specific horrors she had read about in the press over the years; children raped and mutilated, their broken bodies tossed in ditches by the roadway or wrapped in newspapers like gutted fish. It was consoling, but not by great measure, not enough to keep her from going limp on park benches and in the middle of a movie or in the course of a meal in a restaurant.

Everything in her was dead, except the flowing tears. These are the sorrows that take your life away, first bit by bit and then with great stunning blows to the heart; no sea and horizon line, no painting or music, no meal, no sex, no walks hand in hand, no new kid gloves, even if they fit perfectly, can shield you or long console you. So much for wisdom, art, and its vaunted serenity—she would explain that to Professor Morin one day.

She expressed these thoughts to Rex, never claiming originality—that wasn't the point, she said, originality—but she had come to appreciate how all the truths of the world were open and unconcealed and waiting for us finally to notice them. That idea, too, original or not, left her little consolation.

Rex had broken down several times in her presence, and who knows how many more times when he was alone or in the bike shop turning a wheel or drinking a cup of coffee. But worse than seeing him cry was witnessing his silences. He pushed his food noiselessly about on the plate and silently lost weight; a thinner than thin Rex silently came to bed at night with a cutout shape for a body. He left for work late and returned early and went down to his café and read the papers including the ads, announcements, listings, and the letters to the editor. She heard no more about his plans for new bikes or their saddles or even the latest shop gossip. He now came home with his hands washed, an act of contrition for the crime of losing a son—or of resignation, not even he could explain. There was no more "Rex and Son, Bike Makers." There was now the Rex who went to work, like any other man who went to an office and who returned home, washed up; like any other man at his desk in a building that piqued the sky.

Kenji was gone and Rex, she said to him, as if to another person, was going as well, evaporating before her eyes, and leaving her alone to fend off her own sadness. Did not her sorrow count? Was she not also needing consolation? Of course, he answered, as if suddenly awakening to his neglectfulness, but returning all the same into the silence that curtained him from her and from everything else that occupied the room.

Seeing that Rex could not stop himself from vanishing, she one day decided to take on the business of life—as she ironically put it—for the both of them and to force herself outside of her unhappiness for as long as she could bear it alone and find ways to distract him—them—from the event that had crippled their lives.

She proposed a trip to somewhere not Europe or America—to someplace unfamiliar, trying, and difficult, where they would burn down the day with the sheer effort of travel and where the novel locale would follow them down to their sleep and occupy their dreams. He would leave it up to her, he said; they would go wherever she chose, even to Antarctica. It did not matter to him because wherever they went, he said, Kenji would not be there.

That was a good idea, she thought, to sail down to the end of the earth, where the dead piles of floating blue ice and flat sky banished all thoughts of bikes and cafés and green park gardens. She made the arrangements and bought the plane tickets to Patagonia and the ship berths which would follow but at the last minute Rex begged off, saying after a prolonged silence, he would rather not budge from Paris, where, who knows, one day, purely by chance, he might come across Kenji and his abductor walking in the street.

Now she was back with herself again, without the distraction of caring for another, the usual route of virtuous self-abnegation which holds one's own life in temporary suspension. She thought to make a careful plan about her next steps and where they would lead her and eventually, them. For inevitably time would heal and bring them together again; the trick was to aid the process and be ready, at the healing's end, to start life anew.

A French friend, an editor she met from time to time for a Kir (she had so few friends in Paris, she realized, her life there deliberately circumscribed by Rex and Kenji), once said to her apropos of her husband's infidelity and the hurt it had brought her: "You Americans believe that everything can be repaired. Maybe through therapy. Your magic for everything.

"Yes, Dominique," she continued, "but we Europeans know better. To be well fucked, *bien baisée,* is the only cure for what grief life presents you."

But she did not believe that or in the magic of therapy either. She had been fucked often and well and she yearned for

it again; to have Rex enter the bed at night—his voice low—
and spread her thighs in the green light of the café—how long
ago was that?—and then the slow churning, until the stars
went out.

But no amount of day-and-night lovemaking would ever
blot out Kenji's memory. His face to the sky or to a clock on
the wall: "Dat." And, later, when he grew older, to his book
when he saw her approaching: *"Maman est là."* Perhaps, even
now, she hoped, he was carrying his book with him.

He had been welcomed on his occasional visits to the shop
as a little prince by the mechanics. More the prince because he
rarely spoke, rarely showed discomfort or boredom, standing
apart and watching his father move about the shop, talking and
inspecting the progress of the bikes in construction. Standing
serenely apart or sometimes seated in a chair, his hands folded
on his lap in the pleased manner of a schoolmaster observing
his class deep in their books.

"Perhaps Monsieur Kenji would like a newspaper?" Alain,
the shop's previous owner, asked, smiling and turning to the
men in the shop to see whether they appreciated the joke.

Kenji replied courteously that he had no need for it: "The
world," he said, "is the world."

"And," Alain said, with a mischievous smile, "I suppose that
life is life."

"As you say, monsieur."

Where did he get such notions? Pronouncements saved
from the oracular and pompous by the unassuming manner of
his delivery, by an almost comedic raising of his eyebrows and
shrug of his shoulders, a gesture imitated from neither her nor
Rex. From where? An ancient movie with Fernandel, an

American's idea of a comic Frenchman with baguette and beret? Yet there was nothing comic in the somber tone of the boy's voice.

A voice, so unmodern, one that spoke from long ago, when in Port-Royal, Pascal sat in his room, the window arched to the stars and the cold spaces between them that he said had chilled his soul. The same unmodern voice from the century when Poussin found Death lurking in the dark foliage of Arcadia.

She herself had been a child of the seventeenth century, from where everything she loved had come. What else gave density and beauty to modern life as Shakespeare's blinded Lear and his wise fool; Cervantes' extravagant Quixote and his lunatic truths; and without Couperin and Bach to turn music into a philosophy of melancholy and joy. Everything of value in the modern Western world—her world—had sprung from them, even Kenji.

To return to work seriously and fill her days with thought and writing, while being alert to Rex; she was sure that was the route. No more Poussin for now, or any other scholarly work or any book written with publication in mind. One day, in the next millennium, Kenji might resurface, like a man thought drowned, only to shoot up from the sea naked and with no remembered past—and perhaps no memory of her. She would return wholly to her book of fragments, her anecdotes of poets and artists—such as the one about Gauguin she almost read to Rex long ago in a hotel room in Tangiers— events which she felt were the most wonderful and most dreadful in the twentieth century. It was a journal of what had mattered most deeply to her in the modern world and thus a book to let Kenji discover who she was.

She would write it, if only to imagine him, one day, with her book open on his lap, saying, *"Maman est là,"* finding in what she had written her love letter to him. And so, one afternoon, she went to the Palais Royale garden and sat on a bench under the early April sun. The grand Bibliothèque Nationale, where she had spent so much of her studious youth, was meters away, hovering behind her like a giant mausoleum.

She wrote by hand on an old-fashioned yellow pad: "For Kenji," and beneath that a line from Pascal: "Lord, teach us how to sit." Then she continued for some hours, not pausing for lunch or coffee, jotting down names—Cézanne, Rilke, Pavese, Babel, Pollock—of artists and writers she would return to in telling her story, until she finally grew tired and took the Metro home.

There, as she turned the key, the door felt lighter than usual, and the hallway quieter, as if carpets were muffling the parquet, which was, as always, cleanly bare. With Kenji gone, the apartment sounded hollow, as if the furniture had been removed or had never been moved in. She had been growing accustomed to the sense of living in a noiseless shell with windows but now the shell was even more silent and more hollow than usual.

Not that anything had changed physically; every chair, sofa, lamp, table was in its place, just as when she left in the morning. Even the white roses she had bought the day before were still there in the glass vase on a stand by the bed.

"White roses," Rex said. "Don't you know that's for funerals?"

She did know, of course, but she was not thinking of the symbolism when she passed the florist and saw them coolly waiting for her behind the refrigerated window. For a moment, there in the street, she had the mad idea that the roses would be the charm to bring Kenji back and she went in the shop, not even asking the price, and took seven—her good-luck number—and returned home to plant them in water.

Everything was in its place, clothes hanging in the closet, the umbrella in a rack in the hall and the creams, cosmetics, bottles, box of cotton in the bathroom. But Rex's worn-down toothbrush and the half-filled tube of the Rembrandt toothpaste she had bought for him had disappeared. And Rex along with them. His letter in an envelope, resting against a sugar bowl, both announced and explained his flight.

# CHAPTER 19

S EVERAL MONTHS AFTER she returned to New
York and the university where she had taught before her
long stay in Paris, she was cornered in her office by three of
her younger colleagues. They were concerned with her lack of
perspective on departmental matters, as they related to its
patriarchal power base, and they were concerned with her
teaching ideas—or lack—uninformed by those theoretical
currents of gender studies most valuable to students, women
especially.

Once, in class, Dominique had said that there were, as yet,
no great woman painters, their entrance and—reluctant—
acceptance as artists not really beginning until the later part of
the nineteenth century. A group of four students reported her
to the chair as saying that there were no great woman artists,
as if she had been implying that there never would be. What
Dominique, then, deemed scholarship was in effect fodder for
a white male canon at once racist and sexist, and thus subtly
damaging to the younger and more vulnerable—especially
female—students' sense of self-esteem.

She thought for a moment, standing there, her briefcase still in hand, behind her desk, her coat on her shoulders, of reviewing for them the case she once made for an examination of the Western canon before it was yet under its fullest siege. To redress, as would any sound historian, the wrongs of omissions and to discover and bring into view those artists neglected for nonaesthetic reasons in the critical discourse.

She had been proud of herself when she made that little speech to a group of fellow graduate students and junior faculty at her university, years before such ideas were institutionalized and used as a key for advancement. And where she once would have welcomed these colleagues, she now balked at their intrusion. Left fascists, she wanted to say, but she suspected they were not even that. Just power brokers with an altruistic facade.

Perhaps, as was being claimed, she had become a fossil, like her mentor, Professor Morin, who shuffled in the university's corridors living in the glow of past achievements and whose focus remained steadfastly European and formalist. She, at least, had begun to enter the Modernist period and was smitten by some American painters—bound, however subtly, to the great classical tradition whose engine she believed and wished to prove was Poussin. Finally, she imagined that in the eyes of her detractors, her interests were not much of an improvement over her mentor's.

She told Professor Morin about her office visit. She was agitated in spite of her desire to seem cool and above the fray.

"Given that you are who you are," he said, "what is to be done?"

She laughed. "That's what I came to ask you," she said.

"Win the lottery," he said. "Then disappear into your life."

"I'll go out and buy a hundred for you," she said.

"Dominique, you're in America now, no socialism. Buy me a ticket and I'll buy you one."

He looked so old and tired when he said that and had an expression so tender of her that she impulsively kissed his cheek, then hugged him.

What could she do? Lottery apart? She would have to accept her unwillingness to change and take the consequences. She admittedly was outdated on the recent argot of her discipline, refusing, for example, to write "herstory" for "history," as had become convention in certain academic journals, but she was certain that finally, what women wanted was less theory and more change. Stuck in platitudes, with a language governed by slogans and inner-circle rhetoric, the Old Left had infected the language of gender politics. She one day hoped to write about that, the diseased language of the Left. One day.

Dominique was lunching with her old friend Rose at a glamorous uptown restaurant. They had been together several times since Dominique's return, but Rose had made this occasion seem of special importance. And so after a glass of wine, and a few inconsequential exchanges, Dominique let Rose take the lead.

Rose, the once perennial medical student, was now a doctor and an oncologist to boot, her career had stayed on the ordained path, but now there was an addition and a surprise: She had become engaged. The man in her life, Robert, had finally emerged from the wings; in her case, from the operating room. He was handsome, of course, a splendid surgeon and a man of broad cultural interests; they were to have a substantial wedding—Dominique would be her bridesmaid, naturally—and a considerable life of work and children, house and home. Everything solid and in its place, everything that made life not just a mission to endure.

"I want a life of complexity," Rose said, "but without too many complications. If you know what I mean."

"You'll get what you want," Dominique said.

She wondered why she thought that whatever Rose wanted would never be enough for herself. Never deep enough or intense enough. She once would have said "original enough" but she was no longer concerned with that notion; a life could fit any known theme or plot and still be original and exciting at its core. Like a Poussin painting or a Shakespeare play.

That sounded a bit ambiguous, patronizing, maybe; as in what you want is so ordinary that you will be sure to get it. So she quickly added, "Your dreams, Rose. You'll get your dreams," feeling that the addendum itself was not much of an improvement.

"I knew what you meant," Rose said. "Or at least, I think I did."

Sharpness of mind. More than anything else, perhaps even more than beauty. Most were like old knives in a drawer, doing their blunt jobs when required; a scalpel was not needed to slice bread. Yet, however much she prized it, that special sharpness was tiring; she never worried she would tire of Rose in that way. It was mean but comforting for her to think that Rose's capacity for happiness was governed by a mind just serviceable enough to carve her life into functional, comfortable compartments.

She caught her reflection in the glint of the silverware: That she, whose own life had grown so diminished, could still consider Rose's as the lesser only proved her folly and self-delusion, and she saw the star of her condescension and imagined higher being sink into the sea.

They had ordered impeccably, the waiter observed. He approved of them, as if it were they who had planned and soon would cook the meal.

*"Vous avez bien choisi,"* he said, withdrawing with a slight, professional bow.

Dominique had impressed him with her French and with their choice of wine and now everything was smooth and settled until coffee. They laughed, the two of them. The pretentiousness, the lofty menu and its commentary; they laughed at their snobbishness at enjoying the chic table and its accompanying show.

"I would have chosen a good Italian restaurant," Rose said, "but I know how much you like things French."

"Was it a good trip?" Dominique asked, wanting to sound interested.

"The best. A sort of carefree pre-honeymoon. We drove and drove and stopped wherever and whenever we felt."

"How lovely."

"If the hotels were booked—too bad—we just drove on."

"Like vagabonds," Dominique threw in. With credit cards, she wanted to add, but stopped herself.

"That's right."

Dominique had a doctoral thesis to read and two lectures to prepare. Suddenly, the lunch, its price, the conversation, and its cost in time and expense in words overcame her, but she tried to suppress her impatience, which nonetheless Rose presently sensed.

"I didn't mean to go on," Rose said.

She was being mean-spirited and jealous of Rose and that

was the cause of her impatience. A settled professional life, complete with a man equally settled, was something she did not have and perhaps, from the evidence of her choices, did not want—yet did want more than anything.

She was happy for Rose, she said; Rose had earned her happiness and, to use an overused expression, deserved it. She thought of Hamlet's warning to Polonius: "Use every man after his desert, and who shall 'scape whipping?" She was certain Shakespeare had meant women, too.

"You deserve a great deal, too," Rose said sympathetically. Too sympathetically.

"I have what I want," Dominique answered tersely. "Most of it," adding the qualification so as not to seem far-fetched and defensive.

"Do you still want him?" Rose asked.

Him, who? she wanted to say.

"Him? No," she answered. "That's really finished this time. And don't say like the last time and the time before that, OK, Rose?"

"Well, if that's true, and I hope it is, I wonder how you'd feel hearing about him."

"I'd feel fine but I'd rather not."

"Great," Rose said. "Even if you're lying twice."

They laughed. Lunch arrived in its predictable order. So all there was left to contend with was the annoying screech of Rose's knife on plate, and the occasional fluttering and billowing of the beige window curtain in the room otherwise hushed and cushioned by a creamy beige carpet. A pleasant dining experience in an elegantly subdued atmosphere, just as the Zagat had foretold. But Dominique was burning with curiosity and wondering how long she could hold out. Until coffee was ordered, or after its arrival? After the first sip?

"Your patients must think you a good doctor," Dominique finally said after the poached salmon had disappeared from both their plates, "because you appear so calm and in control, so fucking knowing."

"What is it you'd like to know, for example?" Rose asked with feigned innocence.

"The works," Dominique said, reaching for an ancient pack of Camels she sometimes carried in her jacket pocket, her hand feeling the security of its being there, like a little bomb she could throw at herself.

"Are you sure?" Rose asked solicitously.

"I'll tell you if it starts to hurt. Then you'll stop, like the good doctor you are."

"Of course," Rose said. She had had time to mull the story over and trim it to its essentials, she said.

# CHAPTER 20

T HEY WERE IN a small harbor town on the coast of Mexico, Rose began, searching for a ferry to take them down to Veracruz—as a lark. Robert was off to the port and she was just strolling the town square alone when she saw him sitting at a dirty table under a tiny umbrella whose shadow barely covered the coffee cup in front of him. Every so often he'd raise his hand to shade his eyes from the sun, which was baking the day. He went hatless and wore no sunglasses, just him and the hot brightness. She decided not to stop and not to get embroiled in the hellos and exchanges that would follow; she decided that.

But he looked so alone, so lost, and so in the right place all at the same time that curiosity got the better of her and she went over and casually plunked herself in the chair opposite him, hoping in some way to ruffle him.

"Hi, Rose," he said, as if he had seen her an hour earlier.

In some way she was flattered that he had remembered her name after all the years, so she calmed down and, if not ready to like him again, she was not too ready to dislike him, either.

He had the saddest eyes she had ever seen in a man, yet his smile seemed genuine and his demeanor serene.

"What do you mean, saddest eyes?" Dominique asked, her heart suddenly feeling sad in spite of herself.

"I sometimes have the unhappy professional duty to tell people they are going to die," Rose said. "Imagine that. I still can't. I have seen all kinds of reactions—defiant ones and crushed ones—most just collapse into a grim depression right in front of you. But Rex's eyes, to go mushy on you for a moment, they were another kind of sadness."

Eyes, Dominique thought, that had witnessed the sky wedding the evening in a leafy Arcadian wood, where the world reveals its sorrowful face in the color of a green field. In the background, a mourning shepherd pipes melodies he has gleaned from the cosmic whirl, while ancient columns silently crumble in the rosy distance.

Poussin should have painted that; she would have taught him how to do it: Kenji. Were Rex's eyes like that? she wanted to ask.

"He has many faces, that Rex," Dominique said with a forced little laugh.

"He asked about you, right off," Rose said sharply. "I said you were well and teaching again and rather happy. I didn't tell him you were alone or broke or anything like that," Rose continued. Rather meanly, Dominique thought.

"And then?"

"Then the oddest thing. He asked would I come back to his digs."

Dominique tensed up, so visibly that Rose added immediately: "Not for that. He wasn't in that mode."

It was close, a few steps away, and it would mean so much

to him, he said. So she went, thinking to return before Robert
had finished booking passage.

A small room in a depressing small building. His one window faced a sliver of sea. A mattress on the floor for a bed and
nothing much else, unless you include a cane chair, a wobbly
pine table, and a crumbly bureau. The sink was loaded with
flowerpots stewing in a bed of water; an espresso machine
with a charred handle leaned against a pan of milk, the mini-
fridge quivered under the sink. It shocked her how sad the
whole business was and how lonely he must be.

"Don't worry for him, Rose."

He was, for the moment, just drifting along, taking odd
jobs. He didn't want to crowd his day, wanting, among other
things, time to read. She saw no evidence of books in the flat,
though, and she commented on it and he laughed, saying what
a good detective she was. No, he had a friend, a kind of mentor, who lent him material from time to time and he read in the
parks and cafés on his days off. He was sort of rethinking
things, he said with a charming smile.

"My heart went out to him," Rose said. "What happens to
a man like that, Dominique?"

"Who knows?" she said, wishing that she did.

"I asked if he would mind my lending him some money. I
couldn't not ask, seeing him like that."

"Why would I need money?" he answered. "It's not money
I need, anyway."

"Of course, I wanted to ask just what he was doing for
money, but I didn't have the nerve." He went to the baby
fridge and took out a packet of envelopes. Letters for
Dominique, kept safe from the humidity, maybe ten or twelve

of them, unstamped and unaddressed. He wanted her to be his courier and deliver them. Yes, she would do that.

She took the bundle and shook his hand at the door. Good luck, Rex said, *muy buena suerte* or something uncomplicated like that. He took her hand and held it for what seemed to her an inordinately long time. Then he said, in a voice almost stern, almost implying she had pilfered them: "Rose, give me back the letters."

She was about to protest but his tone was so firm she obediently handed them over and left, and that was the end of that, though his presence haunted her the rest of the trip and she could not shake it, even in burning Veracruz with Robert.

The waiter had come and gone with two rounds of demitasse, and then presented the bill, which, to Dominique's relief, Rose picked up. Finally, there was a strained and silent parting at the corner. What to say? Even as Dominique was about to enter the taxi, what to say? Goodbye, Rose, and thanks for lunch. They kissed, they embraced, they promised to meet soon.

Now that Rose had shed Rex's presence, it came traveling with Dominique in the taxi and took up residence in her small apartment and looked out of the window with her at the children splashing in the wading pool and at their mothers chatting happily on Tompkins Square Park benches. The presence slept close to her in bed that night and woke with her at dawn, when she lit a cigarette and inhaled slowly and exhaled slowly and said, "Rex," and then the word "Kenji" before crushing it out and returning to sleep.

# CHAPTER 21

S HE WOKE TO the telephone and the news that Professor Morin was in the hospital. Heart attack, stroke;
everything all at once, if she understood rightly. He was in a
bad way, terminal in any case, whatever the cause. He had
asked to see her. She would have gone anyway, flown from anywhere, but he was in New York and she sped to the hospital.

At first, he seemed quite well, better even than usual. The
shock was to see him in pajamas—striped, like his twin pin-
striped suits—which made him seem naked—or nude? For a
moment she had forgotten the classic art historical distinction.

"What's up, Samuel?"

He smiled a weak smile and waved a hello. He looked old
and drained, the *élan vital*, the life force, as he called it, seemingly bled from him.

"You don't need to go to all these lengths to get me to see
you in pj's," she said.

He always liked it when she did the hardboiled routine; very
American, like the noir movies he loved, where the waitress
called the police detective "bub" or just plain "mister." He

once told her that the smoking chimneys at Belsen and Auschwitz had shown him the emptiness of old Europe's respect for hierarchy and tradition.

"I have tried everything else," he said.

"I don't think so, mister; there's a lot left for you still to do."

"I'll take up that challenge when I leave here. But I'm not leaving here, Dominique."

"That ironic thing you do to ward off a single reading of your meaning, how does it work in painting?" she asked.

She had succeeded in making him smile his rare, unguarded smile, that carried with it no irony, only happiness and self-forgetting.

"We'll take that subject up for your next book," he said. "There's another coming, no?"

"You always say that as if asking, 'Are you expecting another child?' "

"Well?"

"This one's for you, like the last one," she said.

He waved his hand as if to say don't bother, or thank you, or both.

"I left you my library," he said very softly, turning away from her. "And some other things."

"I have a small apartment, Samuel. So please don't inconvenience me by dying."

He laughed at that, as she had intended him to. A weak laugh, caught by a spasm in his chest.

"Which reminds me," he said, "of some last-minute advice I've wanted to give you. If you don't mind my being frank on this ludicrous occasion."

He was caught in the spirit of the jocular moment she thought she had created. She encouraged him to continue.

"Give up Poussin, he's not for you," he said evenly.

"Sure, why not," she answered, still thinking he was joking with her. "I'm moving on, anyway. I'm trying to find the twentieth century." She said it lightly, realizing how pretentious and overreaching her project would sound, and feeling guilty, too, that she had said the book was for him, when it was inspired by and meant for Kenji, her bridge to him after death.

"You've done very good work, superior, I might add, but I think it's time to let go."

"Why, is there nothing left to write about him?"

"I just think you should give up trying to crack him."

"It's funny you should say that now, after I've spent half my life writing about him," she said. She began to sink under his disapproval.

He must have seen her chagrin. "No, no, don't misunderstand. You've done wonderful work. Find someone more generous, is what I'm trying to say."

"Samuel, what and who are we talking about?" she asked, wondering whether he had lost his train of thought or whether age and illness had affected his usual lucidity.

"Who do you think?" he replied, with more affection in his voice than she had heard since their separation in Paris many lives ago.

He was leaving her his library and a few other little things, like his never before expressed admonition that she take up a new life and leave Rex on the shelf.

She hugged and kissed him twice before leaving, then, after taking a few steps out the door, she returned, wanting to give him a last hug. He had seemed to be waiting for her.

"How much time do we have, after all?" he asked, with a shrug.

When she returned home, Rex's presence glanced at her and retreated elsewhere; he did not follow her to her desk, where she was writing a letter to Professor Morin. She wanted to draft it as an essay, "The End of Gentleness." Someone had written that civilization is what you have when no one is looking; she wanted to add, "what you keep even when there is nothing to lose in giving it up." Nothing in these times appreciated gentleness, and little in the universities promoted the scholarship which embodied it.

In Professor Morin's world there was no power play or envy of position, but the notion of a mutuality and exchange of ideas for the sake of thought. A bit on the lofty side, but Professor Morin himself was not lofty.

To the detriment of his career, Professor Morin had never taken sides and never curried favor—for himself. He was passed over by others with inferior scholarship and poor teaching, but she had never heard him complain. He did what he loved and the rest was luxury. The administration eventually gave him a Distinguished Professorship but only when it was clear he was being courted by several prestigious institutions.

University departments, she once said to Professor Morin, were the microcosms not of the intellectual but of the political world.

"Why not just of the world," he added, with a smile and a Gallic shrug.

She wanted to write to let him know, finally, what she had understood of him, and how even though she could not attain his intellectual and moral level—and perhaps she would not try—his example had nonetheless impressed itself on her for life.

A week after Professor Morin died, she received a letter from the dean saying her contract would not be renewed. She had already lost her tenure after her years in Paris, and on her return Professor Morin had used his prestige to have her reinstated, but she had to do her tenure run over again—with reassurances that she probably would be granted it early.

She always had known that in spite of her publications and her ever growing reputation in certain traditional circles, without Professor Morin's protection she would be powerless, and now she was. She would have to face the humiliation of job hunting and perhaps even confront the dreary prospect of being forced to leave New York.

She had become a provincial, as were most who had adopted New York City. The rest of America westward was a large beige space dotted sporadically with striving regional museums and plucky universities. She would have to go to one of those little places and except for the summer trip to Europe and an occasional visit to New York, disappear from everything that had made her life her life.

Two other letters in the mailbox took her away from such gloomy thoughts. Two of the dozen, no doubt, from Rex's trembling fridge, but she could not guess which one from the date. One, written a year earlier, was filled with references to other letters yet unsent or tardy in arrival.

A line, stuck in a paragraph of incidental chatter—so it then seemed—spoke to her as if, in fact, it had a voice. Rex's sweet one, reserved for gripping her. "I miss you, sugar." And then, several lines later: "Are we still together, Red?"

The second letter was more concrete, referring to some news in yet another previous letter. He most likely was on the way to Morocco. Did she remember Ali, their old neighbor and sometime chauffeur? His brother lived in Mexico and had become his teacher. He suggested Rex go to Fez to study with a Sufi master and shed his thoughts of the world and its painful attachments. He would try to do so, but he would not seek, however, to rid himself of her or thoughts of her or Kenji, because that was not possible, nor would he wish it to be. But he would try to comprehend the spiritual truths of Sufism and to find under its canopy the serene shelter he so much needed.

She read the passage twice, put the letter down, and went to the kitchen to make coffee. She drank two cups standing and dumped the third in the sink. The letter was still there on her return, the famous inspirational passage, too.

She would laugh at the absurdity if at the bottom she did not feel pity for his despair and the extravagant paths it had driven him—Rex leaving Marx to search for peace in mystical texts burning with longing for God.

Once, when they were still living above the café, she returned home from grocery shopping to find Rex sitting at the kitchen table. She was surprised to see him home at lunch hour, when he was usually working in the shop and eating a sandwich on the run. His eyes were moist and he looked pale. She thought she should be frightened.

"What's happened, Rex?"

Nothing bad had happened, if that was what she meant. He rose to kiss and reassure her.

"I was picking up a wheel," he said, "and I thought of you and Kenji." It was more than a thought. A wave of love and sadness, like a beautiful fever, passed through him, and he had to leave the shop. He had no idea of why it happened just then, just that it did.

"I sat here waiting for you and wondered what it would be like if you never came back to me," he said, his eyes glistening again.

"Never came back from shopping?"

"To the café that day, when Kenji and I were hoping you'd return."

"Aren't you glad I did, Rex?" she said.

"Where would I be if you hadn't?"

She had wished he had answered differently, wished he had said outright, "Of course, Dominique," or "I would have gone crazy if you hadn't."

"You tell me," she said.

"I'm a failure without you and Kenji. Maybe I'm a failure anyway."

"Oh! Rex," she said, "don't say that. Don't think that."

"It's true. I see it better now that I'm happy."

Even if it were true, she thought, she found his failure more beautiful than another man's success. She kissed him and unbuttoned his shirt and led him to the bed.

"My failed man," she whispered teasingly. "My failed man, who is my life."

"Who could compete with such a troubled phantom?" Professor Morin asked her, at lunch one day, after she had returned from Paris and had related to him its catastrophes and Rex's flight.

"His heart is broken," she said, coming to his defense. "Of course he is troubled."

She deliberately skipped over what Professor Morin had said, feeling that the key to his seemingly disinterested observation was the feeling of his own invisibility in the face of that phantom. She might defend Rex to others, from pride, if little else, but this time he had finally done the unforgivable.

He had deserted her, unforgivably, in the Paris apartment that was their home; he had abandoned the Paris workshop that had produced his extraordinary bikes: All the business matters, salaries, rents, bills, taxes, and paperwork of a mutual life just was dropped—as if from the sky—into her lap.

Trite expression but accurate. Heaps of folders and sheets of *fiche* piled on her lap as she phoned, one after another, those connected to their little world.

She called Rex's partner first, though it made her stomach sick to confess to Eric her failure, her stupidity. She was certain he would think her ridiculous in having chosen Rex over him; Eric, she imagined, never would have left her, at least not in the way Rex had. She had spoken to Eric on the phone a month earlier, when he called her from his plane, flying over Arizona, where he was buying tracts of land. The conversation was friendly, as always. She reported the news of the shop and the mundane events of her daily life. He never inquired about her life with Rex. Now she would have to bring him into it. She felt pained for him, and guilty for calling him when she needed help, but there was no way to avoid informing him about what had happened.

He did not gloat—as she would have expected and maybe had deserved—unless he had become so suave in covering his feelings on the short notice of a second—though she could never conceive of any American being suave, reserving in her mind that role for European diplomats and other professional smoothies.

Eric didn't waste time with expressions of commiseration

and he placed no blame on Rex. As for the business, his lawyers and representatives would handle the matter of its dissolution as they had its conception, and help take, if she wanted, other concerns off her mind. Off her lap! she wanted to say.

She did not refuse his help, which now that she had returned, however temporarily, to his orbit, facilitated her eventual repatriation—shipping, storage, plane tickets, and taxi to her apartment included.

# CHAPTER 22

YEARS LATER SHE would learn, but not from Eric, that the bike business had been racing at a loss from the first moment the first wheel was set in place: No amount of sales at the rate the bikes were manufactured could ever cover the overhead, materials, and cost of labor, and still yield a profit. And she would come also to learn that the sunny apartment overlooking the Parc Monceau had been subsidized as well. Eric's money had carried them, three years earlier, *en famille*, across town, from a tiny walkup above a café to a two-bedroom bourgeois palace, complete with concierge, porter, and an elevator that regularly went up and down.

Rex had left her but not without a strange hope—against her better judgment, and even against her wish not to want such a thing—that he might one day redeem himself and rejoin her.

He had written of such possibility and desire in the letter forever resting in her mind against the blue sugar bowl in the Paris kitchen. He had been floundering even before Kenji's vanishment but was trying to maintain the fiction of his happiness because of what she and the boy had meant—and still meant—to him.

He was proud of his work, he continued, and thought with satisfaction of the small but elegant accomplishment of designing an object of some beauty and function. Not the physical, mortal bike, of course, but its lasting conception. Kenji, he hoped, would one day be proud of his father's legacy—and maybe she, who cared so much for imperishable forms, as well.

Yes, there was pride, but after the initial success of actually making the bike and seeing it spin away, his involvement grew less and less. His idea from the start never was to turn out these bikes forever. To go to the shop every day and do the same thing every day! Yet he would have done it or maybe eventually would have found something else to absorb him, and keep him grounded, because of his love for her and Kenji.

Just to write the boy's name and see it so solidly on the page made him weak. Nothing in his life he imagined could have hurt him as deeply as Kenji's disappearance, not even her death, which would, along with his grief, be a natural part of their life together. He could even imagine the day when she would be dead and the anguish he would feel. But Kenji was neither alive nor dead, and he could not bear the grief of that.

After he was sure that Kenji would not reappear, the bikes and the shop and the whole of the life they had constructed blurred before his eyes and even though he kept rubbing them to return them to focus, they never did.

It was cowardly what he did, leaving her in the lurch. It was not the Rex she loved and who loved her who was leaving her; it was the unhappy man who needed to cure himself with fresh hopes in new corners of the world. He knew she would be able to manage all the details he had left behind. They were just surface matters she could blow away like smoke and were not at the marrow of their life. Everything and everyone except Kenji that stood between them was just smoke, in any case, and was bound to blow away, leaving them to themselves.

"Anyway," he concluded, "we are together. Say that to yourself, Dominique, and know that it's only a matter of time before we reunite."

That was the end, finally. She was not angry or surprised or sad, she thought to herself. It was just another moment in her life and there would be others. She thought of practical things to do to fill in the next five minutes of her life.

"Maybe," she said to herself aloud, "I'll water the orchids."

But she sat there in her kitchen with her yellow pad and began to scribble until she noticed it had grown very dark and her hand was still making circles and loops on the same page. That was Paris and long ago.

Rex was off to Fez. She was happy for him, in a way. For her, there was the prospect of exile to the greater America, now that the reality of the dean's letter overtook Rex's. There was the semester to finish—and the new book to continue, the one she had dedicated to Kenji on a bench in a Paris garden— and then her salary would evaporate, her little savings dry up, and she would have to begin the great pilgrimage to Ohio or to Texas with their universities' endowed minarets pointed to God.

In fact, she would not have to go to Texas or Ohio, but to a version of them in New York State, where she had been offered a professorship with tenure. It came with a two-course-per-semester teaching schedule, travel and research money, and for a nominal rent, a small house with library and built-in bookcases. They were also offering more than twice her former salary.

It was amazing how easy things were when you were wanted. Further refinements to the offer would be considered, should she wish. Of course, for form's sake she would have to come up and present a paper to the faculty and meet key figures in the department, but all that was routine.

There were two other serious candidates, she was informed by the head of the search committee after her arrival, and he was in favor of neither. But she was not aware until lunch that he himself was in little favor with the department and that his proposing her was considered the last gasp of the moribund old guard who had held sway there, as elsewhere, for fifty years. Which explained why her reception that afternoon was correct but not cordial and why when she came to the cozy amphitheater to deliver her paper, the audience of faculty and graduate students seemed sullenly polite, with the convince-me air of a parole board.

She read from an essay in progress on Pierre Puvis de Chavannes, whom she regarded as the pivotal and transitional figure from the traditional French Academy to Modernism. He had gone from being the most famous European artist of the late nineteenth century, who commanded the highest prices in the world for his murals—a million dollars in 1890 for the fresco at the entrance of the Boston Public Library—to being dismissed, if not altogether forgotten.

Modern scholars, she said, should wonder at the low estimate of Puvis, when Gauguin, Van Gogh, Toulouse-Lautrec, had admired him and had admitted to his influence in their letters and referenced him in their paintings. These artists had seen in Puvis the most contemporary example of the order and logic of Poussin but with a palette shockingly novel; his pale roses and blues and luminescent whites hinted of an art at once academic yet subversively in alliance with their own innovations. He haunted them to the end.

Even artists no less than Picasso, whose Blue and Rose paintings were mothered from the pastel shades of Puvis's late murals. Incidentally, she added, Puvis had befriended the Postimpressionists when few did, even hosting a banquet to fund Gauguin's last sojourn in the tropics. A rare generosity of spirit, she said in an aside, didn't they think? The essay grew more technical after that. The silence in the room formed icicles about the edges of her words until she was finished.

Why was she interested in a white male European artist when there was so much to examine elsewhere, especially in the art of the Developing World, people of color, women, gays and lesbians? The question, Dominique recognized, came from a distinguished culture critic and professor known for her early work on Courbet. Beautiful work, she had thought.

She was interested, Dominique answered, because this art moved her and she enjoyed exploring its rich precincts. She would hope to excite that interest in her students. She was not being exclusionary, she added, or bracing up some idea of a canon. Let all art—all creative expression—contend freely.

Some days after she returned to New York, she received a phone call from the chair of the search committee. An official letter would follow, of course, but he regretted to inform her—off the record—that she would not be hired.

They had decided on—with full approval of the graduate students and faculty—a video and performance artist; a frequent contributor to leading theoretical journals, she was famous for her feminist militancy, demonstrated by her having appropriated dominant-male diction and using it in subversive contexts.

"Suck my dick," she had exclaimed to a well-known art critic, who on a panel made light of her video art, and "Sit on my face," to another critic who had similarly offended her on a cable arts program.

"They were proud to get her," the chair said weakly and with an air of a man standing on his lawn alone, watching his garage go up in smoke.

# CHAPTER 23

TWO WEEKS TO the day of the phone call, the official letter of rejection arrived, crisp in its envelope. Along with it and with the usual bills and announcements, a very official envelope from a lawyer's office with four names.

Who was suing her? she wondered. Perhaps the university for having exposed both students and faculty to her retrograde, Eurocentric interests, perhaps, even, in a lax moment, she had said "his" for "his or her," thus forever distracting the students from their studies.

Untangling the legalese, as much as she could, she found she was being advised that until further notification outlining the particulars, she was to have deposited into her bank account a monthly sum, later to be defined, for as long as the conditions allowed.

Would she please contact the office and provide it with her bank routing number and other specifics. It was a joke, of course. But who would play it? She phoned the office and gave the information as requested and received no further information from the paralegal, who in any case probably had no more information to give.

In her dream, admittedly adolescent, it was Rex, suntanned and turbaned—returned from a fabulous voyage, his barque laden with jewels and gold taken from a pirate's treasure buried in a cave in Araby, wherever that was—who had come to rescue her. His treasure first; he, with scimitar, to follow.

Impossible, naturally; Rex was more likely rowing in the galleys than commanding the wheel. Professor Morin had had hardly enough money to keep one of his two suits dry-cleaned the same week he went to have his thinning hair trimmed. The only person with money she knew was Eric, but why would he provide her with an income?

It was hard to believe he was still interested in her after all these years. He had been involved with a socialite for a long time, and they were always photographed as a couple in the society pages. Rose had met her a few times at charity events for her hospital and had reported her very handsome, very athletic, like a runner or rock climber, and not at all horsy.

"Does he seem to love her?" she asked.

"Hard to tell," Rose said. "He wasn't falling all over her, in any case," she added.

Dominique had had lunch with him several times since she had returned from Paris and he had invited her on two occasions to accompany him to museum openings. She had wanted to ask, when he phoned, "Where is your girlfriend?" But apart from the impoliteness, she reminded herself that he never mentioned Rex, discreetly leaving to her whatever remained of him in her life.

In the times she had been with Eric, he was warm, intimate,

without insinuating familiarity, and making no references to their happy days in Paris. She had enjoyed herself with him and was sad when, at the end, he left her off at her building, his car taking him back to his life and to the woman she presumed he shared it with.

Once, just after they had descended the ramp at an opening at the Guggenheim, she left him standing alone for a few minutes. She had gotten slightly dizzy from the descent, she told him, and she went to the rest room to splash water on her face. She stood before the mirror, water dripping from her cheeks, frightened at what had seemed the return of the familiar symptoms of her old illness.

She composed herself and returned to see him circled by people. He was talking, with a grave face, she thought, and was looking darkly handsome—handsomer than ever. For a moment, she regretted she was not on his arm, where she seemed naturally to belong. He beamed when he saw her approaching and kept smiling until they were alone again.

"I was worried," he said. "You seemed gone quite long."

For an instant, she thought she saw his old love for her, when he long ago kissed her hand in a Paris park and asked, "What is the world? What is its joy?" In that instant, she wanted to say, as if answering to a subdued hunger: I've been gone for too long, but now I'm back. But she did not know whether that hunger had come from missing him or missing Rex or from the sudden and returning fear of dying—again— that had come over her before the mirror.

There was still something active and unresolved between them. Yet all his solicitude and the vestiges of his former feelings did not add up to his giving her an income for life. Finally, she phoned him, not sure whether it was to ask about the money or whether she just wanted to see him, and decided it was for both.

It was odd how, in the week he had not returned her call, she thought more about him. Where was he that he could not call back? Was it possible that her allure had vanished? she asked, laughing at herself. She disliked the vanity but she justified it by telling herself, "Lighten up, Dominique, you're only human."

He had phoned her several times, he said, when he finally reached her. But the phone had just kept ringing. Didn't she have an answering machine? Of course not, she answered, quietly relieved at his discomfort at not finding her. She had no answering machine, answering service, fax machine, voice or e-mail; a telephone was enough concession to immediacy. For normal communication there was the post.

"But you called me," he said, laughing. "Remember?"

"I have forgotten why," she said.

"Anyway, I found you."

"Well, what are you going to do about that now?"

"Make a date to see you, naturally." He laughed again. Then added cheerfully, "Somehow I feel this call was set up for me to ask you that."

"Ask what?" She was enjoying herself, bantering with him. He was liking it, too—all the better.

They finally got around to it, the dinner. She had come into some money, she said, waiting for him to take the bait and tell all, but he didn't, so she was inviting him out this time. A great idea, he said; he'd be sure to eat beforehand so as not to tax her budget. She told him that she was glad to find he was still somewhat of a charming idiot. He strived to please, he said, as a parting farewell. It was good all that bantering and flirting, her ego needed it.

Instead of dinner in New York, they flew to Madrid. When he phoned again to confirm their dinner plans, she mentioned in passing that she had not been to Spain in a long time.

"It would be lovely to see it with you," he said. "Especially the Prado, as long as you didn't lecture me too much."

"OK," she said, thinking they were joking, "I'll take you to dinner in Madrid."

His personal secretary phoned a few days later with the arrangements.

"Tell Mr. Wynan," she said, "that everything is Dutch treat, except for a dinner."

"Not the Ritz again," she said, laughing on the plane. "Didn't we settle that business the first time around?"

Sure, he said, but as a backup he had reserved a room at another place, her kind of hotel, with summering professors and students and zillions of other earnest folks, only a half hour away from the Prado by speedy taxi and maybe under an hour by bus. But moderately priced, with continental break-fast—roll and coffee—included. She could stay there and he would go to his kind of joint. Her choice, of course. Of course, from the point of view of time, it would be easier at the Ritz, which, as she knew, he said, was next door to the Prado.

It was only for some dinners and a little trip. She did not plan to make love with him. She felt comfortable that he would not press her—he never had—and was sure that although she found him increasingly attractive, she would not—crudely put—put out for his money. No one had asked her to, she reminded herself.

There was the Prado again. It had been a long time between visits, and though she had lived all those years in not too far away Paris, it had seemed far away because she was absorbed with Kenji.

One day she would have taken Kenji to the Prado to see the Goyas and would wait on his opinions, as he had opinions, sometimes slowly revealed, regarding most things, even about Poussin, whom he stared at for some minutes—longer than most—in the Louvre one fall afternoon, the sky slate and cold.

"They are beautiful, Mama," he said. Adding, "But I do not like them."

"Really," she said. "And why, my little wise man?"

"*Elles sont tellement mortes*, Mama" he said. "They are really dead."

As perhaps he was now. Dead. His body turned to powder; his little voice stuffed with earth.

They took adjoining rooms and met for breakfast. They went across the road to the Prado to devour pictures until lunchtime, then went to their rooms and took siestas in the burning afternoon. In early evening, they returned to the Real Academia or to the Prado and lingered over the paintings they had visited that morning.

"By the time we leave," she said, "I won't want to see another painting for months."

"For days," he corrected her. "It's me you won't want to see again for months."

"Twelve, at least," she said, teasing, yet wondering whether she had actually meant it. He was good company. She wondered whether she was.

They dined late at the hotel, she not wanting to go afar or to do much after a day of museuming, and they caught up on their lives—his, since she knew so little of it, she said, feeling slightly guilty that she always had been the taker of the two.

It was interesting, his life; more than hers, from the point of view of its arc. Her limit was not to be interested too much in any one's life apart from its narrative. A narrative detached from the person, like a story when it floats up from the page, leaving the book behind.

His will was strong and he had used it to take himself out of poverty. Many had done the same but his instance was notable for the distance he had traveled from that poverty. Not comfort, not wealth, not luxury but richness surpassing richness and ever, ever growing. But the dank smell of his childhood poverty never left him, she thought.

At college, she was amazed to learn, he had been a Trotskyite—the word and its meaning seemed so far away, like the name of a nearly forgotten Christian sect before the consolidated homogeny of the Church—and he had believed in the inevitable and perpetual revolution. But he was also an anarchist and hated all manifestations of the state and its—or any—authority.

"You were just a mixed-up kid," Dominique said, "weren't you?"

"That's only half of it," he said laughingly.

She hoped for the moment he would not fill in the other half. She knew enough of his old life and was curious about the new.

"And what about now, Eric?" she asked.

"Well, I'm thinking about getting married," he said in one rapid breath.

"Let me know when," she said, feeling, without any right, she thought, a stab of hurt. She could hear the hurt in her voice, and she tried to lighten her tone, adding: "Let me know in time to save up for a great toaster."

He took her hand. "Look, Dominique, we'll always be friends. Won't we?" he said.

"Always," she said, feeling it was true, though she also felt she was drowning in full sight.

One morning, after a leisurely breakfast while Eric was dawdling over the *Herald Tribune*, she told him she wanted to see the Prado alone this time and especially Goya's *The Puppet*, a painting that had moved her inexplicably, even when she had first written about it in her doctoral thesis as a young graduate student of twenty-five, many Rexes ago.

*The Puppet* had numbered among the cartoons for tapestries for the walls of royal court and were never intended for public viewing. But Goya did not care. He invested the cartoons with his passion for the joy of simple country life of weddings and hunts and dances under the sky.

She had once loved the "Black Paintings" of Goya's later life, with their surrealist adumbrations, modernness of look, and intuition of the twentieth-century world of horrors. But she had always felt that they were easily read pictures, explicit in their emotional darkness and leaving little formal mystery.

Goya was the love of her impressionable youth. One of the reasons she abandoned Goya to write on Poussin was to mature intellectually by tackling work more obdurate, implacable. Work less filled with grounds about which the scholar could expatiate on the human condition, which generally came to mean some simplistic social or moral truth—the human nature business, she termed it once to Professor Morin, who was amused.

She was pleased to have impressed Professor Morin with her newfound intellectual maturity. But that was not why he was amused, he said. It was her enthusiasm, he said, so sincere, and so unself-knowing, if she did not mind his speaking frankly.

"Unself-knowing?" she repeated, at the same moment imagining he had meant her loving the ungiving and the distant in life as well as in art and both with equal unsuccess.

"Do I hear an echo?" he asked, playfully looking about the room.

From the middle distance, *The Puppet* seemed a charming painting by Watteau or Fragonard of bucolic and frivolous French court life. Five young women were tossing a life-sized clothed mannequin into the sky; the blanket which catapulted him was clutched tightly in their hands, ready to receive his fall. The women were neither highborn nor peasants, but somewhere in the rustic middle. Of all the Goyas in the museum, this one now moved her most.

The life-sized mannequin dressed in a blue-green waistcoat and rust-red britches, his face a rouged white mask, flew in air, head twisting to the sky, and long arms hanging heavily, like a rag doll. Everything spoke for a happy, playful scene, and everything spoke for an indescribable—because she could not describe it—sadness.

Melancholy, pathos, sadness, such easy words and, like the inert mannequin, indefinable, like the ineffable feeling the painting gave her when she allowed herself to read it personally. Goya's painting did not illustrate a sentiment but had, she felt, objectified a sentiment buried in her.

"Sure," Eric said that evening over a drink. "I see why you like that picture. It reminds you of you."

She gave out a short, defensive laugh. It was clever what he had said, but was no more original than saying: We are all puppets; it's the human condition, after all. But at the bottom of her reasoning, she sensed he might be right.

"What part does?" she asked.

"The whole show," he said. "You, and the ladies and the puppet."

She stiffened. "Well, how exactly does it remind me of myself, the whole show?"

He heard the defensive and irritated edge in her voice, and tried to soothe her, his own voice going tender. "It's not a criticism, Dominique."

She looked at him, studying his eyes over the rim of her raised wineglass, and found nothing of mischief or mean-spiritedness there. And she waited a long moment before saying, "So, then?"

He inclined toward her slowly and took her free hand. "You are the beautiful puppet, and you are the ladies who send him into the air. You're having fun tormenting the self you keep beautiful and dead."

"That's very poetical, Eric, more poetry than psychology, if you don't mind my saying," she said, offended to be called beautiful and dead.

"It's not psychology," he said, "it's intuition and common sense."

She began to study his face, as if she had not looked at him carefully before. It had more volume than she had before seen or remembered. Perhaps as with that character in Queneau's novel, experience had begun to round out Eric's dimension. Some sadness in his face reminded her of Rex, and some knowingness—if not wisdom itself—there made her think of Professor Morin. But Eric had what neither had, an energy of hope.

# CHAPTER 24

H E NEVER BROUGHT up the subject of her allowance—as she called her windfall—she sensed he wanted to leave it permanently away from them, having said, clearly enough, "That's old business." What, then, was the new business, if there was any between them? For the moment, they had planned a day trip to Toledo to see El Greco's *The Burial of Count Orgaz*, but she was indifferent to the place and to the artist.

"First he was just not much," she said, "then he was discovered by people who wanted to fit him into their Modernist canon and from there on he was the forerunner of Expressionism or whatever it was they were selling."

He was bemused. "Well, I was just curious, you know, to see it," he said. "I wasn't aware El Greco had been taken up by a marketing conspiracy."

She was in a rotten mood and his being charming and attractive wasn't helping it. He had been kind, too kind, too understanding, and she longed to provoke a quarrel.

"Every racket has its gimmicks. I'm sure you have yours.

Academics and critics make them up as they go along, don't you see."

"Well, let's just not go," he said evenly.

He wasn't going to bite; he did not provoke.

"With all that money you've made, you must have some killer instincts. I've never seen them, Eric—do you hide them from civilians?"

"Wow," he said. "That's a leap."

Where had her anger come from? It had come from his gift and the obligation to him it made her feel, regardless of how she tried to reason that feeling away. It had come from her deep loneliness in the midst of opulence and art. It had come from her being a puppet who wanted to scream. It came from his not being Rex.

She apologized. She really was sorry. But then she wasn't.

"My nerves are bad tonight, bad," she said, wondering whether he could hear the echo of Eliot's line, trying not to play with him but anyway playing with him, stupidly.

To compensate for her bad humor, she proposed that she take him out—on the town—that night and added that should he still like her afterward she would go to Toledo with him the following day and promise to be great fun and a great—did she say that?—pal.

She wore her best, sexiest dress and made herself look—as Eric put it when she went to his room to collect him—amazing. They bar-hopped and they ate themselves silly; especially at a place called Museo de Jamones, the tastiest museum in the world, as it dubbed itself, where at the bar, under the racks of hanging, cured *jamones*, she said to Eric: "Here you find a museum with the most honest aesthetics, because here they are verifiable."

She was getting tipsy. It felt wonderful, that slight edge high above the crowd and voices. He was looking good, she said. Maybe not as good as the hams, but not so bad.

"I still have more curing to do," he said. "Look me up in a couple of years."

Where was flirting taking her? Not to bed, but maybe there. She took him to a bar once famous for its artistic and bull-fighting clientele and most renowned for once having had a drunk Ava Gardner dancing on a table suddenly lift her skirt, drop her panties, squat, and pee.

"The golden stream which golden legends are made from," she shouted above the din Eric found annoying and, he added for emphasis, "seriously unpleasant."

"Frankly," he said, "I'd love to leave."

"Look, you're my date tonight," she said. "If you find something unpleasant then I find it unpleasant, even if I'm having a good time."

"That's the kind of generosity I expect from an art scholar and a great pal," he said.

"Goes without saying. But if you find something seriously unpleasant then I must take measures to rectify the situation."

"I see," he said.

"You do understand?"

"Most assuredly."

"Then let's leave, right away, after a few more dozen drinks," she said.

It was getting late. But not for Madrid, where it never gets late enough, where she had left behind some of her late youth in the small hours before dawn. There was a place she used to go, but she did not recall its whereabouts or name, where she had spent time dancing after finishing dinner at one in the

morning, where she was a bit reckless, flirting away and wondering—as ever—where Rex was and what he was doing.

They took a taxi and she explained her situation to the
driver and then they took another and she explained again and
finally on the third try, the driver needed no explanation and
drove them to a perfectly undistinguished two-story residence
with surrounding white walls and a gate of wrought-iron
leaves and pinecones.

Inside, the lighting was pink and orange; the long bar, where
they hovered while waiting for a table over a glass of mediocre
champagne, swam in blush reds; and the garden, where the
four-man orchestra played and where young couples were
dancing old-fashioned fox-trots, was drowned in powder
blues. They reluctantly shared a table—no others were avail-
able in the thickness of crowded tables—with an obliging couple of undetermined nationality, who kept switching languages
with the waiter.

She was happy. Banal, that, but she had no truer word in
answer to Eric's question.

"Yes, I'm happy," she said. She had wanted to add, "but
don't push it," to tease him but she thought the better of it lest
he misunderstand her. The air was soft, tender, as a poet had
once described it, and she, too, was feeling tender to life, to
him, to herself.

They danced. Not too well. She was out of practice. But he
said she was wonderful and apologized for his not making her
look good on a floor of graceful dancers. They did several fox-
trots in a row before returning to their now vacant table, feeling pleased to finally have the table to themselves alone. She
was swimming with the music and the oceanic night and longing to be kissed.

When the waiter came and asked whether they would mind another couple joining their table, she wanted to say that of course she minded and she was certain Eric would, too, but in the spirit of the same generosity shown them by the table's previous occupants, she said, "*Por supuesto*. Is that all right, Eric?"

And he opened his palms as if to say, "Well, that's life, isn't it?" It was, wasn't it?

The waiter soon returned through the crowd with the couple in tow and seated them.

"Hello, Red," Rex said. "You remember Olga, here, don't you?"

# CHAPTER 25

S HE AND ERIC were sitting in the back of a chilled Mercedes, the air conditioning turned up because in the morning Madrid was already hot and humid. She was slumped down in the cool leather with a shawl over her, trying to concentrate on the dry landscape. From time to time, Eric took her hand and gave it a friendly pat and a smile. She returned it with a sickening feeling.

They drove some ways off the main road and then took yet another smaller road and climbed up a driveway of lemon trees to a large white house atop a high mesa. Rex was waiting at the door, having seen them, he said, from his window long before they turned down the road.

He greeted them with a bouquet of starkly white roses he had picked that morning. His crisp shirt was whiter than the roses and contrasted with his dark sunburned neck and face. The sun had tamed his hair, drawing off its fire, which only the night before had burned feverishly. Or was it that she had been burning feverishly in the face of his aplomb, his fucking cool. As if they had just said goodbye the day before and he was meeting her for a drink, as if all their years together had been a mutual dream remembered by one.

Two men came up to them and, with many apologies for their interrupting, spoke to Rex in the most rapid Spanish she had ever heard. Rex answered them with the firm authority of the Castilian *caballero* whose part he looked. The men left, looking relieved.

Some horses had broken out or had been let out of the stable and had been found wandering far from the estate. Out for breakfast, no doubt, Rex explained, with a smile. He was sorry for the intrusion and promised them a peaceful lunch after a short tour of the *finca*, that is, should they wish to see it. She would love to, some other time, she said, because they were a bit pressed to get to Toledo to see some pictures.

"Well, it's nothing grand," he said. "But very pretty, with about twenty thoroughbreds and a stallion or two of great distinction for breeding."

They finally entered the house with its wide rooms and newly cut flowers soaking in the light from the large bright windows. Airy and gracious and marvelously cool with a silent central air conditioning system; the sofas white and deep, the chairs white and deep, the fireplace broad and high, the ceilings high, skies unto themselves.

Presently Olga appeared, in jeans and short boots, like the ones the ranch hands who had approached Rex had worn, except these were handmade of tooled ostrich leather, clean and unscarred. Like Rex, she too wore a white shirt, open far below her throat, her suntan visible on the curves of her breasts.

"*Hola,*" Olga said to the room, with a full smile showing

some crooked teeth. She was no longer beautiful, but she was energy. Olga had made a dashing entrance and Dominique could see that even Eric was, if not smitten, struck.

They had much to talk about or maybe nothings at all, Olga said with a laugh and a toss of her black hair. Like a caricature of a Gypsy fireball, like Carmen, maybe.

How did this all happens? she asked the room. She would tell all at lunch, she answered—and maybes even at dinner should they wish to stay. Stay forever, should they wish. Rex laughed.

Rex was charming; he was gregarious. He commanded the table without bullying it, making certain that everyone was served a second portion—to make the cook happy, he said. He recommended the flan for desert and made sure the after-lunch cordials went the rounds.

He told jokes and made Eric laugh.

"The man from Tanzania says to the man from Kenya: 'In your country you have dog-eat-dog capitalism.' The man from Kenya replies: 'In your country, you have dog-eat-nothing socialism.' "

Dominique saw Olga look at him with shining eyes; he made her world shimmer. She knew that feeling. He was at the bar again, two hundred years earlier, chatting with the French girls and making them believe in America. He was young again, and so too was his diction.

"It was the strangest thing. I had my bag and was ready to leave for Fez and dig the beauty of the Koran, when I bumped into Olga at a hot-chocolate stand in the train station."

"Do you think I would not recognizes him? I always recognizes him." Olga gave a laugh. Then another.

"I loves him from that first time in Mexico, even after he leaves me all alone. Then one day," she said, turning to Dominique, "everything change. My father's brother, the one who stayed with Franco in Spain, one day he stops living and lefts me his lands and his *dinero*." That was a big change, she said, but that came *despues*, after years she had no *dinero* and had to raise her daughter all by herself because some Red gringo had leaves her, all alone, *completamente sola*, in Chapingo, Mexico. She gave Rex a pretend sharp look.

"Well, let's be fair, there, Olga. I left Mexico without ever knowing about the little darling."

Yes, that was true, because it was against her principles to make a man do so bourgeois a thing as to stays with her because of a child. She was no little Catholic girl. And even if she had to says it to herself, she was no *cobarde*.

Eric was amused by her, looked at Olga admiringly, and Dominique felt a little wave of jealousy.

"Life never afraid me, never," she said.

"I'm sure of that," Eric said.

Rex seconded the motion, and then it was time to take coffee on the patio. Dominique felt a tapping on her foot and turned to Eric and seeing no hint of recognition on his face, quickly glanced under the table to see Rex's boot on her shoe.

"Why don't we all take a little walk around the garden before coffee," Rex suggested to the table. She waited for Eric to agree first and then added her approval. Only Olga seemed unhappy at the prospect.

"You stays with me," she said to Dominique, "and we do some ladies' talk."

"Now, Olga," Rex said, "let's all go out and get some air."

Dominique waited for Rex to add the word "sugar" or "honey" or "sweetheart" to the end of his sentence. She was expecting some sweet word to form into a sugar dagger and stab through her heart.

They strolled through a walled garden of roses and cacti; Olga on Eric's arm, taking the lead. Rex, pretending to show her a special flower, took Dominique by the wrist, halting her as the others continued on their way.

"How are you, Red?" he asked. "How is our world?"

She turned from him, her hand shaking, as it had that day when she had realized that Kenji was not coming home with them from school.

"This is just a parenthesis for the sake of the daughter," he added. "I can't leave her now that I've discovered I have her."

"Where is Kenji?" she asked, wanting him to know that the boy was all that was left between them.

"You know where—lost," he answered.

"He had no choice in that," she said.

"That's not fair, Dominique. I'm as lost as he is."

"What if I ask you to leave with me, right now. Would you be lost then?"

She did not know what she meant or if she meant it. Even years later she didn't, looking back on that garden with the sun getting hotter and Toledo seeming further away than Iceland.

"Do you think anything has changed between us? That anything ever could? Do you, Red?"

Olga had turned her head and waved to them. She laughed but her face was not laughing; she tugged at Eric's arm as if to rein him in and turn him about, but he was a stupid or willful horse and kept on track.

"I came here because I forced my curiosity to be stronger than my repulsion," she said. "I'm glad I came. I've enjoyed the show, Rex."

"Red, I just want to stay awhile longer and see my daughter get set up. I'm just getting to know her."

She stared at him and then at the one ripe cloud over his shoulder.

"Give me a year, or two," he said, "and I'll join you anywhere."

"Everyone has these plans for me, five years, ten years. My plan is for two hundred years of solitude."

Coffee was served under a leafy trestle; grapes in bunches hung from the open roof and ran in clusters along the support posts. It made a temple in homage to Bacchus; all that was missing were the happy drunken revelers.

"We never goes out," Olga said. "Rex like staying at home and doing little things, he could do them all days and night those little things." But then she said, "No, tonight we goes dancing, and we do goes and find you."

"What a fortunate coincidence," Eric said. "Just think, we might never have met."

There was irony in his voice, Dominique thought, and why not.

Yes, how lucky that they did bumps into each other, Olga said. Also fortunate was that their daughter, Rosa, was coming home from school at any moment and they would meet her.

"Some other time," Dominique said politely. Because the day was spending itself, and there was still Toledo—which now there was no question of going to, wanting instead to return to her hotel room and scream with rage under a pillow—and the return to Madrid and the flight back to the States that evening.

It was rushed, their departure. Rex accompanied them to the waiting car and shook Eric's hand.

"I've always wanted a castle in Spain. Let me know," Eric said affably, "if you ever think about selling your ranch here."

"Not likely," Rex said, a little stiffly.

"You never can tell," Eric said, with the same cool, unsteadying look he once gave her when she came to propose the bicycle business. "Things seem to change so quickly for you."

His disdain for Rex was chilling. Eric was brilliant, she thought, having waited for his moment, with only her for a witness, to fully appreciate it. And Eric's contempt registered on Rex's face.

Rex said nothing, went around to her side of the door, took her arm, squeezing it tightly, and leaned to kiss her cheek.

"Forever," he whispered.

On the return, they made small talk.

"He's a curious fellow, Rex," Eric said, an hour into the flight to New York.

She did not like his condescending "curious fellow." It was only for her to speak ill of Rex, and since she had not and had not invited him to, she felt he should not have spoken. Still, he was right, and to be fair, she said: "Yes, it would seem so." In agreeing, she also felt she had given him a new power and high ground which she would never again regain.

# CHAPTER 26

I T WAS STRANGE to be living in her small apartment again. She missed the high ceilings and airy space of her hotel room at the Ritz in Madrid—even after several months. Missed the easiness of the everyday, when her bed was made up and dinner was served some stories below in a shaded garden. She even missed Eric, but she did not long for him. She did not miss Rex. She did not miss him.

She was no longer teaching. But she was working at home, in her small flat overlooking Tompkins Square Park. Writing every day in her manuscript for the "Anecdotal Biography of the Twentieth Century," the working title for her journal of fragments and mosaics.

She had been making a list of items she would return to and fill in: the book burnings and other acts of murder by the Nazis; the internment of the poet Mandelstam and his consequent death in a gulag by the Stalinists; the assassination of the elected president of Chile by the CIA. For balance, on the side of creativity, she also wrote: Picasso's and Braque's invention of Cubism; Glen Gould's rethinking, thirty years after the ini-

tial recording, of his interpretation of Bach's *Goldberg Varia-
tions*; Alain Resnais's *Last Year at Marienbad*—his distillation of
images into a cinema as formal as a Poussin painting. She
added these items to a hundred others still waiting to be written. It was becoming an account book of life against death,
hope against despair, at the end of which she would make and
deliver the tally.

She had opened the window to modern times and was letting in all sorts of breezes. She had been writing that morning
on Rilke—whom she did not much like—his *Letters on
Cézanne*. She was moved by the way the poet had loved the
artist's work and how he would travel anywhere in Europe to
see even just two of his paintings.

Not Rilke but his wonder at the depth of Cézanne's devotion to his art moved her, but not more than the painter's
devotion itself. When the very devoutly Catholic Cézanne
received news of his mother's death he did not attend the
funeral because, he said, if he had made an exception for his
dead mother and had broken away from his work where would
the exceptions end?

The religion of art that Cézanne had devoted himself to
had vanished; art had not, but in the vacuum of belief, art's
practice and function had become decorative or worse, illus-
trative of ideas. Even the old myth of the artist's struggle for
aesthetic truth had become a convention in the service of
publicity. No artist went hungry, no one suffered isolation or
rejection, except in the occasional recycling of the myth for its
marketing allure.

And, finally, even the myth of the artist's struggle and self-
sacrifice itself vanished, derided by artists living as princes.
The new myth was of success and celebrity, the same myth

believed by the general culture, in which artists as well as celebrities strove to star.

Hers was the obvious complaint, and as she was reflecting on it she cautioned herself against complacency and smugness, the generational self-righteousness she herself had decried as a youth. Her caution did little good.

It was not wealth or success she was faulting, many great artists had had both, but something indefinable, absent from contemporary culture; she would put it down to a soullessness in the absence of belief. She herself was a materialist who absurdly believed in the soul. As she hoped would Kenji, wherever he was. Loving, always, in body and soul.

Rex was the example of the artist without true belief. He decorated the world, made it attractive and lent it charm—no little thing in a graceless time. Even after leaving him at the edge of the road with his new family and the *finca* behind him and his "forever" in her ear, she could construe his duplicity as a part of his endless complexity. She could ridicule herself for her self-deception, but she could never be sure it was self-deceiving of her to believe in his love for her. She had not expressed it to him or wished to admit it to herself in the broad light of reason, but she still carried the suspicion that at the solid core, there was only the two of them.

The morning mail arrived. Even after relenting and getting e-mail, she was still receiving letters, relics from the mechanical universe, from Newton and his world of pulleys, gears, and cogs. Gallery announcements and bills, the mainstay of the epistolary old order, and on occasion an odd letter from a former student.

But this was from the law firm which had contacted her months earlier. The outline of the early letter was now set out in its particulars. She had been left money, to her surprise, by Professor Samuel Morin, not Eric. The amount might fluctuate depending on interest rates, but even she understood at first glance that with careful management, the income would outlive her. Not a great amount taken annually, but more than enough for someone whose greatest expenses after overhead were books and music and travel.

And some clothes, of course. She had always liked dressing well, a few carefully chosen dresses and a few pairs of expensive shoes ruling the lexicon of her wardrobe. She could now add to it, extend its vocabulary without worry or guilt. Professor Morin had given her a life more comfortable than his had been. His entire—and considerable—life's savings and university pension had gone into providing for her—"For your freedom," he said, in a sealed letter accompanying the lawyer's document.

"It seems I have won the lottery before you did," he began. "So enjoy what freedom my little winnings may give you," he said. "I wish I were with you to see your story unfold; that would be one of the pleasures of being alive. I have never been original, so forgive me, Dominique, if I quote from an American novel: 'Live, live all you can.' "

A monograph more than a letter. He clearly had taken his time in writing it and had given it the finish of much deliberation. He had wanted his words to count, he said, because he would not be present to qualify or explain them to her. In all twenty-five pages, never the word "love," but it was palpably breathing throughout the text.

He had been a refugee, he said, when he left France, and had stayed one all his life in America, saving money against the next disaster, for the next time he might again need to flee. By the time he felt no one was looking over his shoulder with an eye on deporting or killing him, he was already too old to make use of what he had saved. And by then, too, old habits prevailed. Saving and doing without had become familiar friends.

What was he to do with his little nest egg? Leave it to a university?—they'd swallow it up for postage money. To yet another scholarship? To a cat hospital, maybe?

She could see him lift his shoulders as he wrote the last line.

It was not as if he picked her name out of a hat, he said. She shouldn't think that. Or because he had no family—thanks to the efficiency of the Nazi camps. It was that no one else had warmed him over these years.

It was an amazing thing, that this man had loved her all these years, from the beginning (he said, without saying it) when she walked into his seminar on Goya. He tried not to stare at her like some swooning undergraduate; he tried not to make a fool of himself when, in the middle of a sentence, he saw her hair catch fire in the streaming light of the window.

From the start, he had hoped that she would be average, just a good student who followed along and did not too remarkable but adequate work and got the serviceable, job-getting doctorate and disappeared along with the rest who had vanished into their ordinary careers and decent lives.

There are extraordinary scholars, he said, and great art historians, but they did not necessarily have an eye, especially for anything out of their specialty or their period. And then there were the savants, semieducated or autodidact, who in a spin about the room could detect the fake or the copy from the real, and could tell, from among a wall of paintings, which ones mattered.

The joy and the catastrophe, for him, though he did not use

the latter word, was that she had both talents, the scholarly and the critical, and that they were born in her as in few others. Thus he had no grounds to dismiss her.

He had seen her in flames by a window, but it was he who had been on fire, he said—asking her to forgive the stale image. But one day, as he was lifting his teacup, he decided to leave his fire—he was no fireman—alone and to let it burn forever or until it burned out.

From the point of view of its impress, that would have been enough mail for a month or a year, for the remainder of her life. She could now have her mail forwarded to "person unknown." She was, after all, a bit on the unknown side of the street, a woman kept by a ghost.

Sometime after the letter, the books arrived in crates, shipped to a room in a warehouse near the East River, where she could walk to easily and handle the riches at leisure. He had winnowed down his library to five thousand volumes. Thousands of others, along with his diaries, journals, and correspondence, he had bequeathed to a university library in Jerusalem. He had had a golden reputation in Israeli intellectual circles and for years had meant to take up the various invitations to teach or simply to reside there, as his presence was considered pedagogy enough.

But the years eased by and he never went. Now his mind would be housed there. One day she would go and sit in that library, where he occupied some space, and discover, in the way that only his writing could reveal, who he really was.

"For church I have the museum; for God I have art; for the oceanic, there is music," he said, offhandedly, once in class. For ethics, he added, he had Kant. She would have said: For ethics, he had a good heart.

Eric had one too.

One week after they returned from Madrid, Eric took her to Saint-Saëns's *Samson et Dalila*, an opera they both loathed, but they had been too polite to tell each other so until intermission. Soon after which, like guilty truants, they fled to the Algonquin Hotel. Supper revived them but the brandies afterward brought them down again. She looked about the room in that hotel legendary for the famous band of wits who had drunk there and made their memorable cracks. She expected their eminent ghosts to be drinking there now, as she supposed her spirit would one day be bothering a café with a green glow.

"Would you like to take a room here tonight?" he asked casually, after they had finished their second round of brandies.

"What would your girlfriend say?" she asked teasingly.

"I only see you here," he said.

"I'm not so tired that I can't make it to a taxi," she answered.

"I can see that," he said.

Then he looked about the room awhile. Suddenly, he motioned to the waiter and ordered another round of drinks without asking her.

"Unless you're tired," she said. So much depended on that word once she said it.

The hotel was tired with its stale tradition and tired carpets, and she was tired of her own story and its chronic repetitions. And Eric, she was sure, was growing tired of her, as he well should be, since she was exhausted with herself. He shut his eyes for a moment—so untypical of him; his eyes, she imagined, remained open even while he slept, the better to see all opportunity—then, he reached out and took her hand.

"Dominique, I've been staying awake for years. Haven't slept a wink," he said.

"But, I'll have to very soon," he added.

He had grabbed her by surprise and seized on the unexpected moment, the moment that for her weighed more than all their time in Madrid and as much as the hours they spent under an elm tree in Paris.

"Are you going to get married?" she asked, sinking unexpectedly at the prospect.

"Not that I exactly want to," he said. "But for her it's now or never. You can understand that, can't you?"

"Yes," she said. She did.

She imagined his girlfriend—his fiancée—in full riding costume atop a stallion: "Now or never," she said, digging her spurs into her horse's flanks.

"Where is she, anyway?" she asked.

"Where? She's ready to move on, is where."

"Where tonight, I mean," she said.

"On Tuesday nights she does charity work at a hospital. I like that about her," he added.

"Do you love her?" she asked.

"Not the way I wish I could," he said. "Not the way it counts."

"So what then?"

"You know," he said. "Do I have to spell it out? It's time for us to move on, too."

"I really didn't know you still felt that way about me, Eric."

"Of course you did," he said.

"Did what?" she asked. They both laughed.

"Anyway, we're not talking about what I want. The ball's in your court where it's always been. Unfortunately," he added.

"I could love you," she said. "I was starting to once, in Paris. I've been starting to again here, but maybe that's because I thought you were getting married."

"That's an excellent reason," he said.

"You know what I mean," she said.

"Too well," he said, laughing.

"I've been happy these weeks with you," she said. "In Madrid, too, until that stupid night."

"Don't you think we should try? Isn't it worth trying, Dominique? How much time do we have, after all?"

"I've just been lucky so far," she said, rapping the edge of the wooden table.

"I'll take my chances."

"You'll take your chances?"

"We'll take our chances," he said. "Stop correcting me, Professor."

"You've never seen me after chemo," she said. "It's not a party."

"Don't take this news badly," he said, "but you've never been much of a fiesta."

"I'll tell you what," she said. Tell him what? She herself had no clue as she said it, but the plan mysteriously revealed itself to her while she was speaking.

"I want," she continued, then she corrected herself. "Let me see him one more time, and after that, either way, it'll be final."

"That's very flattering to me," he said, with a little ironic shrug of his shoulders. "But, let's be realistic, that's how it's always worked with us."

"Well," she said, beginning to object, but finally found no grounds to.

"But on the tally side, there's you," he said.

"For what it's worth," she said sadly, feeling she had let him down.

"For the great value to me," he said.

"I wonder about you sometimes, Eric," she said, brushing her lips lightly on his mouth. "How did you ever get anywhere with your sensibility?"

# CHAPTER 27

S HE HAD TO do all the work, as usual. Writing him draft after draft to find the right tone, until she realized that there was no right tone. To save face, to keep her pride, what rhetoric could manage that for her? She had hit upon the simple lines "Need to see you. This matters."

Eleven days later he answered with: "When? Where?"

Not Spain, she thought, which was now his domain; and not America, now hers. But Paris, where they once had shared a common ground and where their happiest selves still lingered in the streets and sat at the tables of their old cafés. She wrote Rex the particulars.

She was going away for a little while, she told Eric. She kissed him. Not more than a week, in any case, she promised. She herself did not know. Two days for travel and one hour or a night with Rex.

At the worst, she told herself, which still had much to offer, she'd patrol the Louvre for a week and be ravished by some paintings and perhaps even come to some new terms with Poussin before returning home, and to Eric with a definite yes or no. Or she would return home with nothing decided, and remain in perpetual suspension, while Eric and his girlfriend moved on and married.

Or she would drown in the cold November rain before Rex ever arrived. Sheets of water running off the café's awning and flooding the street. Soon the Seine would rise and wash over the city, the Sacré-Coeur bobbing like a wedding cake in a giant lake and herself a little porcelain figure atop the frosting and holding on for dear life.

A waiter she had known years earlier spied her and left his station to come to her. He, too, had been away, he told her. His wife, fearing he was growing too old to be on his feet day and night, had urged him to leave his profession and buy a dry cleaning business with the money he had saved over the years and with the sale of his position to a younger man who had dreamed—for the prestige of its name and clientele—of serving at that café.

He did not enjoy his dry cleaning business and had little exchange with the customers, whom he thought ordinary, in any case. But now he was here, having bought back his job at considerable expense. But it was worth it to be again with such interesting clientele as her and her husband and the beautiful boy, who must now be so grown. Would they be joining her?

He yes, the boy no. And he should arrive any moment. But no one was arriving and those who had tried to leave were huddled at the door or bunched under the canopy's waterfall, watching the rain splitting the pavement.

Rex would have to pass through them and she would not be able to see him until he entered the café, giving her little time to compose herself and hide her annoyance that he was late; for the moment, not by much. But from the point of view of showing some contrition for his betrayals, he should have arrived before her and been sitting there—forever—in her place wondering, worrying, whether she was delayed or simply wondering if she would ever come.

She saw a taxi slow down before the café but her view was blocked by the congregation huddled under the awning. She lit a cigarette, returned to her newspaper so that he would find her, if the passenger in the taxi indeed was Rex, absorbed. She did not raise her head to look at the door, although some moments had already passed and Rex surely would have had time to wade from the cab to the café. She did not raise her head until she heard a voice call her.

"*Hola*, Dominique."

It was Olga, her shoes leaking water. She looked down at the table and shook the rain from her raincoat.

"Well," she said with a desperate little laugh, "he has lefts us, he has lefts us both."

# CHAPTER 28

S HE GAVE HERSELF another day or two for the Louvre before returning home. She could make it three, or
even more if she wished; she was free, a woman at large. She
had lunched with Olga the day following the deluge at the café
and it was clear to both that it would be their last meeting in
Paris or perhaps anywhere.

Without Rex who knows what would brings them together
again, Olga said. Rex brings everyone together excepts himself, she added. Olga was jovial at the wake, trying to bring the
lunch to a graceful end before the check arrived. It was elegant, Dominique said, of her to come all that way to Paris, to
meet her, to tell her that Rex had quit them both and to keep
her from waiting for who knows how long, at the café or back
at her hotel, for him never to arrive.

"Oh! He would comes, maybes in a year," Olga said.

Rex was actually on the way to her, his overnight bag packed
and waiting in the hallway, the taxi soon to arrive. He was to
stay a day, at most two or three, and resolve what there was still
to resolve and then maybes return to her and the horses and

the daughter. Just a coffee at the Café des Plantes, he said, and maybe a dinner.

"And maybes a bed?" she asked.

"Who owns persons?" he asked.

In any case, it was not that kind of meeting, he said. They had to resolve the spiritual side of things, he and Dominique, so they both could be free to be free.

And her spirit? Did he not cares for that or did he think she did not have some? Of course, they fight. Meaning she fights and makes a large scene in the hallway so that the servants come out the doors and raise their big eyebrows. She wanted to laugh at the Spanish farce she had created but it made her angry the disgrace she had made in the servants' eyes.

If he left, she said, she would kill the horses. She did not mean it but she could think of nothing else Rex was as fond of, and she shouted it out a few times before he took her by the shoulders and said, "Look, Olga, I won't go to her but I won't stay with you. That's fair enough, isn't it?"

She thought she had won and that he was only trying to save face by pretending to leave her. But when the taxi arrived and took him away in a direction away from the airport, she realized he was abandoning them both and going to who knows where, to what end or to what beginning of the earth.

"Maybe he's returned," Dominique said. "Maybe he's there now."

"He's no there," she said. At least not an hour ago when she phoned. Or the hour before that.

The check arrived. "I owe you a lunch," Dominique said. "Let me take it."

"We are still *compañeras*," Olga said. "Even withouts a revolution. And then," she said mischievously, "we have always shared, haven't we?"

The lunch had left her in an unserious mood. Two Kirs and a Kir Royale had helped lighten matters, and Olga's almost comedic narrative had done the rest. But the mood did not last the night or the following morning when, as she entered the Louvre, a melancholy came over her, as if she were alone and would always be alone. Alive and wandering among walls of art, she felt dead among the dead, until she found Poussin's *Narcissus and Echo*, leading her back to the living world she had always known.

Beautiful his body, naked but for a red and a white cloth about his groin. Narcissus seemed to be sleeping, on the bare ground, under a sky rich with blue. The luxurious sleep after lovemaking, the deepest repose of youth and health, of the beauty that enchants the world and leaves it in longing and disappointed with its own ordinariness.

He had looked at himself in the still forest pond and without recognizing it was his own beautiful reflection mirrored there, fell in love. Narcissus had thought the divine form had surfaced from its dwelling in the pond's depths to greet him, and, trying to embrace it, he drowned. His death a case of mistaken identity.

But she always had believed Narcissus had realized it was with himself he had fallen in love—at first watery sight—and the understanding of the impossibility of ever uniting with this divided self made him die of loneliness. That was how Poussin must have interpreted the myth, or else why paint Narcissus sprawled dead by the pond's edge instead of drowned in the water deep below.

In the background, the figure of the nymph, Echo, wasting away, dying of unrequited love for Narcissus, who had died, one might say, of similar cause. Dominique could say the same of herself, she who had been similarly mortified by rejection.

Ovid turned Echo's bones into stone and transformed Narcissus into the flower later given his name. Even in his metamorphosis, Narcissus had gotten the better part of the deal, his transformation into a flower bringing beauty into the world—and thus forever receiving its love—while Echo stayed fixed in history as the boring redundancy of voice. Narcissists always triumph, she thought.

To the right and slightly above Narcissus's prone body, baby Cupid stands, torch in hand, his eyes coyly averted from the scene of the twin deaths, as if to disavow responsibility for the mortal wounds he had delivered with his capricious shafts of love. But Dominique knew that, like gravity, Cupid had neither shame nor guilt, causing, without reflection or purpose, humans as well as the world to tumble and stars to vanish into the pool of darkness.

# CHAPTER 29

IT WAS NEVER a choice, life or art. That was just a literary idea. When she and Eric were building their new home on the Montauk cliffs, she did not think: Now I will give myself to life, to its supervision and management, as if life were independent of career and were in itself a calling to follow.

It was just that when she returned from Paris and met with Eric to give him her decision—leaving out entirely the story of Olga and the café, leaving out wholly whether she had met Rex for their decisive meeting—she was thinking already of projects they would undertake together.

As they walked beside each other, arms to their sides, down the asphalt path along the East River, bridges looming, she asked:

"How may I spend your money?"

"As you wish."

"Is that just a manner of speaking?"

"It's what I want," he said firmly. Too firmly, because he added in a softer way, "It's what I would like."

She did not want any money for herself, she had enough of that for what she cared for and for how she had always wished to live, give or take a few amenities to facilitate the day.

A tugboat passed. It seemed she could reach out and touch the line coiled at the stern. She could hop a ride, take to the sea and leave the world she had known behind. As Rex had done countless times. Last chance, as the tug seemed suspended waiting for her—now or never.

She went to her new life calmly and with a certain detachment, as if an agent for another party, the other self she was ushering into being. She wanted Eric to buy the house and property her parents had been forced to vacate and to buy the land adjacent to it, as much as he could obtain, so that she would see no house and no person within her peripheral ken, so that her domain and scope was house and sea and sky.

He laughed, pointing out that, as she well knew, others had bought and were living—if not exactly in her parents' old house, which had been torn down—on their site in a Postmodern plantation manor with many gables and chimneys. Of course she knew, but she expected that if he had as much power as everyone always assumed, the problem of the present tenancy should be easily surmountable, and maybe even afford him some pleasure.

"Don't you like winning?" she asked.

"If it's for you." He was looking about, impatiently, she thought.

Perhaps he was expecting from her something more romantic, more feelingful for him, but she was not disposed to that, and perhaps less now than ever because she wanted it all sorted out, clear and agreed upon, before the next phase of their lives took hold and habits were formed.

"For me? I'd say that it's for us in the long run."

She wanted to create no grounds for future regrets and mis-understandings.

"Well," he said, "as long as you have your list out, why don't we cover all the items."

He was talking to her as to a valued employee seeking a promotion. She could feel his impatient indulgence and wished that she had not brought the metaphoric list but it was difficult to pretend, at that stage, that she had never had a real one.

"Help me," she said. "Go to the ends of the world and find Kenji for me. I don't care about the rest."

Even the giant house she had built high on the cliffs with a view of sea and sky but sequestered from sea and road, blind to the world. The giant transparent eyeball she had asked the architect—the architects, for there had been several, all of whom she found lacking and finally banal—to create for her, so that the atmosphere, sea, clouds, surrounding trees, wheeling seagulls filtered like light through the house. It was all the nature she wished and all that she could bear—too much unspoiled, natural life reminded her of Kenji and how he would look at the sky and sea and screaming gulls in wonder.

To leave the house when she chose, she constructed an underground library and gallery to house her ever growing collection of drawings and some few paintings. "The icebox," Eric called the subterranean building. With the protective lighting and optimum temperature to keep the art from deteriorating and the books from mildewing in the seaside humidity, she had constructed the perfect shelter for everything left in her care.

She did not include herself; Death, she knew, could penetrate her fortress as easily as it could her flesh. Ever since her first bout with cancer, she felt it there in the shadows. A sensation of weakness and exhaustion would sometimes come over her in the course of the day, regardless of the hour or how long she had slept the night before. Death would come sooner or later; she hoped not before she had some word of Kenji.

Dominique's underground sanctuary, Eric once said at a dinner party, was Poussin in concrete. In a way, he inadvertently had hit on something. Coolness that generates warmth was Poussin's format, his method and his essence. Poussin would have appreciated her bunker with its high ceilings, whitish-gray concrete walls spaced with paintings, redwood floors carpeted with Moroccan rugs the colors of red clay and golden beaches. The paintings, as she was quick to point out to the very few visitors she allowed into her private domain, belonged to her husband, as did the house and everything it contained.

Largest among the seven canvases on the walls, a huge Roy Lichtenstein *Interior*, the very one she had written about after her return to New York, the artist's work renewing her interest in contemporary art.

In no other living artist had she found such an inheritor of what was once called the Tradition. Lichtenstein had absorbed the Tradition in the rhythm and placement of his images—the chairs, sofa, coffee tables, and mirrored walls of his painting, speaking for a classical ideal of aesthetic and emotional unity. Lichtenstein was Poussin without the narrative, and like the Frenchman he took life's stampede and tamed it within the borders of canvas.

"Oh, blessed rage for order," she said lightly, paraphrasing a poet she loved and in answer to why she had built the bunker and had furnished it so starkly and with so little art when she had the world of paintings for her choosing. It was the Senator who had asked, a man of some charm and intellectual scope who had opted for politics after abandoning poetry and law.

She had invited him to her bunker only after her husband let her know that it was impolite and not politic not to do so, as the Senator several times had expressed more than passing curiosity in visiting her preserve.

The Senator laughed, pleased, she thought, to have caught the reference to Wallace Stevens. "She sang beyond the genius of the sea," the Senator quoted, letting her know he recognized the poem and had enjoyed her confidence, and that he could play her game.

He was an attractive combination of culture and power, one that she found in her husband as well but found rarely again in the many deadly evenings of black-tie dinners, cocktail parties, theme lunches—with an occasional imported Moroccan orchestra—for sixty on the tented terrace overlooking the ocean.

"It was perfect," Eric said after such a lunch, complimenting her for her role in making it such a success.

"The lunch was perfect," she repeated. "But not one word was said from the heart."

Who was she to judge? Writing her "Anecdotal Biography of the Twentieth Century" was curiously out of line with how she was now living. What perspective outside of comfort and power could she bring to her thoughts, to her judgments?

Once, in bed, after a small dinner party of eight, in which the conversation had been concentrated among the men—

attention to the women decreasing as the talk grew more and more focused on property deals in Central America—she turned to Eric and said, "If I stay with you, I'll soon believe the world is made up only of billionaires, and that I've always been one."

"It's not such a bad way to think," he said.

He was only joking, he said, after she reproved him.

"Only half joking, anyway," he added, laughing.

The Senator was responsible, through the power of his committee, for immense allocations for the purchase of military hardware, some of which, she was troubled to learn, was manufactured by her husband.

"You're an old Lefty," he said matter-of-factly. "Right, Dominique?"

"I'm an aging old Lefty," she said.

The Senator knew all about her and Eric, he said. Had looked them up long ago, before his friendship with her husband—and her too, he hoped—had begun to solidify. It was better to know beforehand what he was getting into, didn't she think?

She had looked him up, too, as far as his record would allow, but she did not know what was behind the public screen. Was there anything interesting to know about him?

"Nothing," he said, "except some broken marriages and wayward children." Nothing so rich in personalities as in her history.

"Herstory?" she asked, laughing. "Well, give me an example or three of my story." She asked it casually, as if it did not concern her at all what he knew or how he had come to know whatever he knew. It did not matter by what covert means her life had been spread out to him—as if she could not guess. She was just an armchair liberal, he said. No one was interested in her back then except that she was involved with a harmless fellow who hung around with radicals in Mexico and France.

"All that is common knowledge," she said, her heart beating a little faster. Spied on, reported on, put on file, what did she expect? America, doing what everyone did everywhere. Which is why she felt soiled, even while she was pouring the Senator another glass of cold Montrachet in the safety of her bunker, in the political indifference of the sea rolling on the beach below her concrete wall.

"Tell me something new," she said, as if wondering what movie he might recommend.

"Nothing that I suppose you don't know already, Dominique."

About Rex, she wanted to say. About where he was and what he was doing and what he was thinking. About how Rex had made his way to her again through so unlikely an ambassador, though he had always been present—even through these thick walls.

"But if you're wondering about that fellow, I don't know a thing. Now that you're not seeing him, I'd have to check his file separately. There is no need for that, is there?"

"Let's go to dinner," she said, not bearing to answer him directly. "I would love you to tell us how global globalization really is. Care to give us some key?"

The table: five billionaires (in the Hamptons millionaires were becoming as commonplace as housing contractors) and their independently successful wives, herself, her husband, the Senator and his friend, a poet of some success who, everyone knew, was the Senator's better conscience.

Globalization came to the table with the coffee and the

three desserts and stayed for the cigars and the after-dinner brandies. She asked the Senator some questions and, to her embarrassment, repeated one or two of them. Much said at the table had made sense to her for a moment but then seemed to blur in her mind, like news heard faintly from a radio in a distant room.

Dominique, the scholar among the oligarchy: Jack London would have found a subject there, if he had not already written *Martin Eden* or *The Iron Heel*, novels which, when she was young, had formed her views of the rich. Simplistic views, as she was now coming to feel in the mellow candlelight and even more warming brandy.

It was a gracious table, not a crass word, not a rude presumption of power, and nothing so categorical or reductive as the soft voice coming from a green room long ago and far away: "The class struggle was very clear then; it's better covered now." Rex had penetrated the upper house as well as the bunker walls below.

"What will happen?" she asked. "When the class differences grow so vast as to create a virtual caste system, even here in America?"

There was no response. Who was left to respond when she had asked the question after the guests had long left and her husband was long ago asleep in his carpeted and soundproof room? The crash of the sea troubled his sleep, whereas it nourished hers.

He was the best of them, the Senator, better than those guests who came after him, those dozen or so who had found their way—through her husband's intercession—to her cave, dying to see her treasures, and finally, disappointed at its meagerness, eager to report their findings to others on the same social trail.

With all her wealth, couldn't she afford a more grand collection? The question was unvoiced. But someone remembered: Wasn't there a little Rothschild chateau just outside of Paris, where a Titian hung unostentatiously over the fireplace in one of those rooms where people went to smoke a cigar? And in Maryland a couple had built a collection of contemporary masters large enough to be housed in a museum, which, in fact, was what they were building on their property.

"Well, my husband decides on these matters," she said. "They're his paintings."

Which they were, as it was his house, his land, his plane, his cars, except for the Dodge convertible she had bought to bang around Montauk years earlier with Professor Morin's money, and they were, finally, his paintings, purchased, like everything else she had cared for, for her happiness.

"Don't worry, Eric," she said. "They'll only appreciate and make you more money in the end."

He was not worried, she knew that. He did not care whether they grew him piles of gold, she knew that, too. But she was defensive about the luxury, the ever increasing life *de luxe*, requiring sometimes that she wear the couture clothes her personal income could not afford, which he supplied on permanent loan, along with the jewelry.

He bought an apartment in Paris, for them. For her to go when the mood struck, when she wanted to live in the Bibliothèque Nationale for a few days or weeks or hang out in the Louvre, like the perennial graduate student she was at heart, a fancy student who made him feel like an undergraduate in love with a doctoral candidate—his words. She did not go to Paris often, and when she did go alone she stayed at a small hotel on the Rue des Saints-Pères, registered under her maiden name as if she might recapture her old identity.

Recapture Kenji, whom she'd find alone on a park bench reading a treatise on the constellations, to explain what it was up there he had gazed at so long at night from his window, his finger pointing to some milky cluster unknown to herself or to Rex: "Dat."

One day, when he was a student sitting on a bench reading Pascal, would he say to her: "The cold between the stars frightens me"?

But most likely, in whatever country, America's influence would reach him, and he would be a boy like any other ten-year-old, disappointingly so. Glued to the tube, roughing it with the other boys, playing video games or baseball or whatever it was that was meant to bring out in him all the manly virtues needed later to compete and to win and to acquire. Just another boy, just another man. Would she still love that Kenji? Of course she would. She did not care if he became a thief as long, as long as his heart was good. As long as he was kind. As long as he was alive.

They had searched for him for a long time. The sum Eric spent on detectives ran into the millions every year, she calculated. He had turned the known world into a grid, broken down to avenues, streets, alleys, doorways, windows. The detectives sifted through cobwebs and recalled whispers, sniffed the school bench he had last sat on, plastered his photograph in metros and buses, broadcast it across the Internet, promised huge rewards for evidence of even the faintest trace of a hair from the disappeared boy.

The police were baffled and would have long ago buried his case were it not for the incentive of a huge reward. Though, eventually, incentive or not, the file unofficially was left to molder, along with the other defunct investigations of all nations.

The private detectives kept on, justifying their fees by pursuing ever thinning leads and investigating even the most farfetched reported sightings—even one in the Bronx Zoo, where the boy was supposedly seen riding atop an elephant. Eric didn't care about the money, he told the detectives, told her, as long as there was still no proof that the boy was dead. There was none; none that he was alive, either. The only certainty was the one that lived in her.

"I have some news about that matter you asked me to take a peek into," the Senator said.

She pretended she had half forgotten that after dinner at her home a year earlier, as the Senator was leaving, she took him aside and said:

"That fellow we were talking about. It would be nice to hear what's happened to him. If it's not inconvenient, George."

He had become George in the course of the dinner; all the intimacy that would have otherwise taken years to attain was compressed into an evening at home because he had become, after all, a man who knew more about her than her father had or her husband would.

He took her aside into an alcove, while the reception milled about them, two hundred gowns and tuxedos raising money for the Senator's campaign.

"He's in Mexico stirring up trouble," George said. He laughed. It was a genuine laugh, from a man who had seen most of life's follies, including his own.

"Started another family or two?" she asked coolly, trying to hide her agitation.

"Hell, no," George said. "He's trying to organize a union in some of the American factories down there, electronics or shoes . . . I forget which. Maybe even one of Eric's plants."

"That would be funny," she said. "One of Eric's plants."

Rex, she thought, had gone backwards, to an age when workers tossed wooden shoes in whirling gears and cogs to break the machines that had broken their lives. Didn't he yet realize that modern capitalism was the new socialism, limed with fresh thoughts and new hopes?

Class interests inform class thinking, she did not need Rex to remind her of that. They were now informing hers, even if only at Eric's secondhand. Long ago she had conceived of a world above such interests, when she was alone facing a painting she loved and feeling its beauty divorced from the world and the artist who had created it or when she stood alone before the sea, swelling to join the sky, herself melting away into the greater universe where the world's struggles were not registered in eternity.

Such heightened moments even her practical father had felt, at night, on deck, his head to the constellations, his body swaying with the sea swells. She could recognize in his voice the little ecstasy that had come over him in the starry darkness.

"Better than church, isn't it?" His voice soft like a child's just woken from a beautiful dream.

She had intended to build a replica—down to the nails—of her father's old house, on its exact site facing the sea. That was one of the conditions of her marriage, to restore her parents to their former, happier state, where they would remain in safety until death. But after her mother died, her father did not want to move, wishing to remain where he felt his wife's presence among the familiar walls and the little patch of rose garden.

She wanted, for the years she had left, her life free of guilt, without Rex's social reminders or his moral example. At the bottom there was no value, principle, ideal, or person worth sacrificing a moment of her life. In the end, there was only the life lived, with its intensity, and its freedom.

# CHAPTER 30

S HE SAT IN the reception room settling down to wait, with six anxious others, the long wait of New York doctor's visits, but Rose ushered her in immediately to tell her that not all the tests were in.

The delay meant nothing, Rose said, her hair in a neat bun, just some test glitches. In fact, the lab promised to messenger the report later that afternoon. But this was Friday at the start of the summer and nothing worked as it should, the weekends beginning at Friday noon. Rose ordered her not to worry.

Years had passed and she thought she had gone free, but Dominique had recently been told that there was a spot, most likely cancerous, on the healthy lung. She now had to face the prospect of more operations and chemotherapy and the prospect beyond that—should those treatments fail—of death, fire, smoke, and ashes—a life that had never quite jelled into a life.

"Will I have time to put things in order, as they say in the movies?" Dominique asked, smiling.

Even at the worst, Rose explained, there was a long way to

go before that. Depending on whether or not the cancer was a new, primary one or was related to the original and depending on what the latest tests showed, they would decide on which among the many new therapies, new treatments, to prescribe. But the tests so far indicated Dominique had years of productive life to look forward to. Although she might have to undergo a course of treatment very soon.

"Did you know Henry died?" Dominique asked suddenly of an old mutual friend.

She had read about it in the papers, Rose answered.

"He was doing his best work," Dominique said. "I was reading his Cézanne book in manuscript the week he died."

She looked out the window where the sky was. Then at a picture of Rose with her tall husband and two adopted Chinese children facing her on the desk. Then at another photo of the children with a black Labrador with a rose between his teeth.

"He asked to be cremated," Dominique continued.

"That's the best."

"Cremation?"

"A living will—just in case," Rose explained in professional tones.

"A few days before he died, Henry asked his friends to carry him down to Southampton Beach to see the ocean. He could hear it from his house—but the great thing was to see the ocean, hearing it just wasn't the same thing, was it?" Dominique added.

"No, not at all," Rose said.

"Immersing oneself in the ocean one last time, that would be great, wouldn't it? Or would that be too much to expect?" Dominique asked with a little laugh.

And so, Dominique continued, if she ever became too sick

to even go down to the sea, would Rose see to it that the end was quick and, if possible, painless?

Rose came up from behind her desk and sat at its edge facing Dominique.

"Don't ask me that."

"Who else, then?"

"I'll think about it. And I'll put that request in your folder. Just for the record."

She was very good at what she did, very efficient, inspiring confidence, Rose, the doctor.

"Well, also put in the folder that it's a matter of professional courtesy, one doc to another," Dominique said with another laugh.

She was Dominique, the doctor, but a doctor of words and not the flesh. Neither lasted.

"It won't come to that, I assure you."

Rose promised to phone her, even over the weekend.

They kissed each other lightly on the cheek, Rose giving her an extra hug—for courage, Dominique thought.

She wandered down York Avenue, the day's brightness full blast over the white mountains of New York Hospital, until she stopped, finally, at a deli, where she bought her second pack of cigarettes in seven years. The other was still sleeping in her drawer. The dromedary winked at her, his lost, old friend returned home to the oasis at last. She put the pack into her pocket, in case; at a certain point, what did it matter if she smoked again?

And now, with the day and herself exhausted, she was returning home. Her car was waiting for her, stationed at a bookstore on Madison Avenue; her driver, Karl, already having stowed in the immaculate cavern of the car trunk the large parcel of books she had ordered. She did not want to take the Midtown Tunnel and asked, even if there was more traffic, to be driven down through her old Lower East Side haunts and over the Williamsburg Bridge.

Once over the river and its watery traffic, she closed her eyes, seeing the afterimage of a green freighter and a green tug make their way to the Narrows. With her eyes still closed, she listened to the Shostakovich Piano Trio—the whole darkness and tragedy of Stalinism was crystallized there, she had once told her students—replaying it until the car sped past Great Neck, when she let herself be overcome by sleep and slept all the way home, dreaming of Captain Nemo and his book-lined cave under the sea.

# CHAPTER 31

S HE HAD TURNED fifty when the millennium was just a year old. "I'm half a century," she said to Eric. "I don't need another birthday party." He was all for a grand event, inviting everyone they knew; she would acquiesce only if he would agree to postpone it until the summer—and then with just a few friends—Rose and her husband. It now was early summer and she was still fudging. She was tired of events, of openings, of parties. Another would not lift her spirits.

Only hearing good news about Kenji would do that. But she had received no news in over a year, the last from a source in Japan, which had renewed her hope. A boy of Kenji's description and age—he would soon be ten—was seen in a park in Kyoto but when the detective attempted to follow the boy and the man accompanying him, both disappeared in a chauffeured Jaguar. The detective had returned to that park several times but never again saw the boy. Of course, there was no certainty that it was Kenji. But there was none that it was not.

She waited sleeplessly on that uncertainty. Finally, she contacted the agency and asked whether the detective had noticed what the boy had been doing in the park. Two days later she received a fax saying simply: "The boy reading book." That was all she needed to keep her hope alive. "It's wonderful news," she said to Eric, "isn't it?"

"Yes, of course," he said. "Wonderful news."

She could hear in his voice the doubt she herself had tried to contain, having received other such wonderful news in the past which had come to nothing.

Even though she slept most of the way home from the city, her tiredness remained, so she took her mail directly to bed with her. Requests for donations from foundations promoting the arts, from museums large and small, from arts projects and organizations, she slid these letters over the edge of the bed. She looked out at the gray sea and grayer sky.

A trawler was slowly crossing her horizon, returning to port, and she imagined herself in it, sorting the day's catch—bluefish maybe—as she had when a child by her father's side, fatigued at day's end, her lungs pumped with sea air, her face and hands filmed white with cold brine.

She sifted through the rest of the mail, tearing up a letter asking her to fund a chair at the university where she had taught and sprinkling the shreds over the mound of letters below the bed.

She froze on coming to one envelope, recognizing the handwriting. She wanted to shred it immediately as she had the other but she longed to open the envelope to stop her heart from pounding. Finally she chose to discipline herself, to control and enjoy the longing a while longer, so she put the letter on the night table, on top of a pile of monographs she was reading.

The house phone rang softly. She picked it up before the second ring, expecting to hear that Rose was on the other line. Her husband had been delayed but had just arrived, Karl announced, and was asking whether she could make an exception and dine at nine?

In Madrid, even as her thesis took hours from her day, she ate at eleven and stayed up to three or four in the morning dancing and drinking, then reading in bed for a few more hours, until sunrise. These days, she finished dinner at seven, was asleep by ten, and was at her desk writing at the shards of dawn, the thick sea bulging in her window. So much for youth and late nights and early mornings to bed.

Finally and without reflection, she took the letter and examined it as if it were a relic of spar taken from the China sea, or a wedge from an explorer's cabin splintered in an Arctic crush—Rex's message to her from his far-flung life.

It was dated four weeks earlier and had been sent first to her old university, where it had sat in the mail bin for retired faculty and others on leave, and from there to Montauk and then to her bed.

"It's been a while since I wrote you," the letter began. "I hope you got my last letter from Mexico."

She had, a letter so pamphletlike and impersonal that she even read a portion of it to Eric: "Because socialism has failed does that make capitalism any less rapacious or more benign? Because many in America and Europe live well, does that pardon what capitalism does to keep most of the world impoverished and under its heel?"

If he calculates a year or more as "a while," she wondered, what would "long ago" mean in his measurement of time?

"But I'm not in Mexico now, anyway," the recent letter continued. "I drifted awhile since then and have landed in Arizona, near Tucson, where I have rented a little cabin on a dwarf plateau in the desert. There's no true road here, only a hard trail, an old Indian path, probably. There's a clump of mesquite and bushes in the gully below and when it rains the flood surges up in a rush, leaving me happily stranded here for days. When the water subsides, red flowers and wild patches of green shoot up from out of nowhere, turning the gully into a fierce little oasis."

"He's turned nature writer now," she said to herself, laughing but not amused.

"Are we," the letter continued, without transition, "still together, Red? Nothing, of course, has changed for me. What is time to us, anyway? All our separations and our being together is the same moment, the time we are alive for each other."

She put the letter down, resenting him again, although she had been sure she had given up that feeling a while ago, as he would say. A shadow spread through her: It shamed her to know so much and to have it mean so little.

Perhaps Rex was right and fidelity took variant forms; infidelity being one of them. Could she consider herself faithful to Eric in their years together, when the sight of something red, a bandanna or a fire engine, could evoke Rex and make her retreat from the day? She had been faithful in her body but not always in her thoughts—did that still make her monogamous, or was she, like Rex, on the shady side of fidelity?

There was more. "I'm having some work and health matters here to attend to, so I can't travel too easily right now. Will you come to see me?"

Apart from its amazing presumption, which she should have long been accustomed to, there was something odd about the letter. The handwriting was unsure, less bold than in the last letter. There was an unfamiliar frailty and shakiness in the hand, which, while altered in its usual strength, was unmistakably his, signature apart. Perhaps he was really ill?

In any case, there was a matter he knew she would want to go over with him. It was very important. He had underlined the "important."

She tossed the letter on the carpet with the pile of others, then picked it up, replaced it in its envelope, and stuck it under her pillow.

She showered, dressed for dinner, and went down to the giant kitchen, where she and her husband took all their evening meals, except when guests were invited—which for the present was mostly never. She clasped a strand of eighteenth-century paste emeralds about her neck and a circlet of the same on her wrist.

She preferred paste's texture and dull green gleam to the shine of real emeralds, as she preferred everything quiet and muted. She seldom wore jewelry except for formal occasions, and even then she often wore none. She acknowledged the luxury of such decisions while disliking herself for enjoying such surplus.

Eric had given her those pastes one day, casually, while they were walking in London on their way to the Victoria and Albert. Took them, wrapped in ordinary tissue paper, from his pocket and handed them to her saying, "Found these the other day, Dominique, they're mid-eighteenth-century, English, I think."

He didn't think, he knew. Trying to sound casual, trying not to make her feel oppressed by the gift, as she did when receiving gifts of any kind. He had learned that about her and he acted on that knowledge.

Her husband was standing by her chair, smiling, waiting for her. He had been away in Paris on business and still wore the tired patina of travel. He bowed to her slightly, then embraced and kissed her.

"What do you think," she asked midmeal, "about our taking a short trip to Madrid?"

He beamed and reached across the table to take her hand. "Depends on when," he answered. "But I like the idea."

"I'll let you know when I have a more definite plan," she said, her voice trailing off.

She was already moving to a new thought and was furloughing the Madrid trip in her mind, where the project decomposed and vanished before coffee had arrived.

"Do you want a break from work, Dominique? We can go anywhere you like."

It was paintings she wanted to see. The Goyas, of course. And not to break from work but to work even harder and longer. It did not have to be Madrid.

He broke into a song from the time of the Spanish Civil War: "*Madrid se bien resistes, Madrid se bien resistes, Madrid se bien resistes, mamita mía, te bombardieron, te bombardieron.*"

"You were too young for that war," she said tartly. "So why all the nostalgia?"

"True. But my mother taught me that song when I was a kid. It's what the Lefties had for nursery songs." He laughed.

"Better fascist than Stalinist," she said ruefully.

"Those weren't the only two choices," he said.

"Well, the fascists killed the Republic but they saved Spain," she said. "Who cares anymore, anyway?"

"You used to, for example—and a great deal, Dominique."

"In my childhood," she said. "These days all the Marxists have gone into business successfully, knowing how capitalism works, as only they do. You, too."

He protested. "I was never a Marxist, darling, just a Trot."

"Gone into business," she continued, "or to universities."

Her voice, with the rest of her, went away for a moment. Where was she? That morning again, at the university when Professor Morin was saying to his class, "For church, I have the museum; for ethics, I have Kant." Isn't that what he had said?

"The universities," she continued, "where they spout the latest fashions. They've funneled Marxism down to the triumvirate of gender, class, and race theory."

"Why don't you publish that in *The New Criterion*," he said, laughing.

"Or maybe we should just go home to Paris," she continued. "Couldn't you use your pull to close down the Louvre and have me live there a week?"

"I'll just buy it for you."

Long ago in Paris, she had warned him never to try to impress or buy her with his wealth. He had taken her advice—perhaps as a strategy to win her, she thought—but after their marriage, even if playfully, he started reverting to old habits, which she did less and less to discourage.

"I don't think I'm leaving the country just now," she said.

He regarded her for a moment and pushed back into his chair.

"What's wrong, Dominique?" he asked gently.

"The condition of culture today. The condition of rivers and oceans and of the whole atmosphere. The condition of our condition."

"No doubt," he said. "But it's you I'm talking about."

"I guess I'm just glum," she said. She laughed at her using the word. "Is 'glum' still a word?" she asked.

"Sure, glum people use it."

He could still be charming—she still found him charming. There was always an imbalance in love—the one who loved and the one who was loved. Most of her life she had denied it, desiring above all a total equality in love. But nothing in her real experience proved her theory—her wish—correct.

"Forgive me," she said. "I just had a bout of self-pity. I carried it with me all the way from the city."

"Let me in," he said.

She told him reluctantly, wishing to be fair to him, about her visit to Rose and how she was waiting for the test results. The fact that Rose had not yet phoned when she said she would made Dominique certain of her suspicion that the results were positive.

"Maybe the reports are still not in," he said, volunteering to phone Rose at home if necessary. "At least that would clear things."

Her husband knew how to confront the unpleasant. It was a quality in him she liked. In a list of calls to make, he once advised her, start with the one you dread the most.

He excused himself and went to make the call.

"Don't try until tomorrow," Dominique said, stopping him. "I'll sleep better knowing nothing."

She wanted the evening to end on that note.

Eric made a gesture, as if to say, As you like; I won't call.

He returned and kissed her hand.

"Nothing bad is going to happen in any case," he said. "Didn't Rose tell you that?"

"Why are you so sure?" she asked suspiciously. "Have you already spoken to her?"

"No, not today, but we won't let anything happen. Not with all the ammunition at our disposal."

"I see," she said, wanting to add, meanly, because death is afraid of the rich? Is that why?

"I know that sounded foolish," he said. "I heard it myself. How can I say this without sounding even more foolish? I love you, Dominique, and I'll put myself between you and anything that comes."

He came and embraced and kissed her. "I love you even more for your bravery."

She kissed his eyes.

Rex's letter under her pillow upstairs was burning through the bed, down through the ceiling, and setting fire to the table. Didn't he see it?

She was thinking of making a short trip, to a conference in Tuscon, for just a day or two or maybe three, she said, from nowhere in herself. Or if she felt bored, she'd come home sooner.

"Would you like me to join you for part of your stay?" he asked.

"Look," she said abruptly, "we're assured, aren't we, Eric?"

"Of course, Dominique. Unless the weather's changed without my knowing it."

By a strange coincidence, there was in fact a conference in Arizona that she had never thought of attending, but which now seemed to give her trip to Rex a certain legitimacy. Perhaps she would attend and not go to see Rex, so why trouble the air? Her rationalization was obvious even to herself.

"I'm going to visit him," she said. "Just a brief hello."

"I understand," he said, his expression somewhat pinched.

"Or maybe I won't go. What do you think, Eric?"

It was a trick question, she realized, even as she asked it. If he had forbidden her to leave, she would have walked through the door and boarded a plane with what she was wearing. If he had acquiesced—"Sure, why not?"—she might read it as his willingness to finally be done with her and her entanglements.

"I can't tell you what to do," he answered.

He never had, and that was his strongest glue.

"Is it that you don't care?" she asked, wanting to pull a definite answer from him.

"Care? I should tell you that if you go don't bother to come back. But I can't."

"Oh! Eric, sometimes I don't see why." Her tears blurred the candlelight.

He took her by the hand and drew her up from the chair, as he once had done at the edge of the last century in a park in Paris.

"We've been fine," he said, "but I've never been in your heart."

She put her hand to his face. "It's not true," she said tenderly. "You're deeply there."

"Nothing in the world has made me as sad as that," he added, not meanly, without accusation and without hope.

I'm your Rex, she wanted to say, as if to soften his unhappiness and to explain to him the logic of his foolishness for loving her so completely.

# CHAPTER 32

S HE HAD DRIVEN a long way off the main highway
and over the winding desert road, and now the day began
to cool. Long shadows patched the mountains and cast him in
bluish shade. He was as lean as ever, even taller and lankier in
his tooled cowboy boots than when she had last seen him. The
sun had faded his blue jeans and his red shirt, even as it had
grilled ruddy color into his face and had drawn years from his
age. He squinted, lines hatching under his eyes.

He gave her a slow smile, a smile that once had made her
forgive him everything.

"Here you are," he said with a little salute.

"Well, I suppose so," she said, with a tightness at the edge
of her voice, surprising her.

He was regarding her obliquely, shying away from her eyes,
studying some prospect or hill behind her.

"Why don't you look at me?" she said angrily. "Are you still
playing games with me?"

"I'm looking at you, Dominique, but I don't see you too

well," he said. "The eyes are sort of going," he said with a little laugh.

She took in his words for a moment, not certain she had
understood what he had said. Not see her too well—a cryptic
and portending remark made from his nervousness or wish to
impress her.

"You're so cool," she said. The last word sounding so old-
fashioned to her. She laughed at herself. He let out a laugh,
too.

"You know what I mean," she said.

He moved toward her hesitantly—so unlike him; he was
only a little older than she but his smooth stride and noncha-
lance was fading with his youth. But then his words returned
to her and she sent out a little cry.

"Oh! Rex." All her fears—although she had tried to resist
them—about his health problems, as he had put it in his letter,
now seemed real.

"Your eyes?" she said.

"It's all right, Dominique," he said, his voice full of tenderness for her.

"God, Rex, how much I've missed you," she said. "How I
still miss you."

# CHAPTER 33

I T WAS A drab room with wonderfully rich bookcases. A
kitchen with one stove and double sink; there were no
dishes piled in the sink. Two cane chairs, their eight legs intact,
guarded the antipodes of a long wooden table. Some pots and
pans and a huge bouquet of dried red peppers hung from a
beam above the table. At the room's center, a large and deep
stone fireplace flanked by windows almost the room's height
and facing mountains and sky. The door at the end of the
room led, she guessed, to a bedroom. She would not spend the
night.

She wondered how she could best let him know her sympathy for him. After all his years of losses and work, mostly for
others, to end up alone without the ability to see, and without
money, was horrible. How small a word for the large universe
of unfairness.

Before she walked through the door of the cabin, she
already thought to give him a portion of her income so that he
could live his life without worry; and would arrange his com-

ing East and being examined by the best New York specialists, who would know how to repair his vision, for obviously the local doctors did not. She would help him recuperate his life in ways neither he nor she for the moment could imagine.

They sat holding hands on a deep brown leather couch, covered with blankets the color of the naked red clay floor. He smiled, and shyly excusing himself, turned to the lamp table beside him, taking something from its drawer.

"Forgive the vanity," he said, putting on a pair of faux tortoise-shell glasses. He had not wanted her, he explained, to see him so altered, wearing spectacles on their very first meeting after some years.

"Oh! God," she said.

"I just can't see at a distance, everything's blurry. Just shapes," he said.

"There's no fool like you in the planet," she said. "Except for me."

He laughed. "What's the problem?"

She was trying to regain her sense of humor. It was odd how in her conception of Rex's life, she had never factored in aging and its diminishments, having reckoned him fit only for catastrophe.

"Well, keep your glasses on long enough to see me leave," she said.

He seemed puzzled.

"Don't you know you broke my heart for a minute?" she continued.

"Didn't mean to, Red. I was just so happy you were here."

Whatever that meant. But she knew what it meant, along with the old familiarity that had taken them only minutes to reach. His words did not fit the meaning, but they had fit her, like his lips.

"Your letter made me think you were ill," she said. "Why the fuck else would I have come all this way to see you?"

He started to speak but she broke in.

"By the way," she said, looking about the room, "is there anyone else here?"

He looked at her quizzically. "Like a dog or cat?"

"Like an Olga?"

"We're the only ones here, Red, and the only ones who ever will be," he said, his voice lowered and serious.

She said nothing for several moments, while the sky darkened and the cactus galloped in the purple shadows, while suddenly she was in the darkening room where they had been all their lives.

She realized that his letter had given her the pretext she needed to see him. It was her illness and not his that had brought her to his door.

She was tired, she said, having waited hours to change planes at Dallas and then having had to drive fifty miles from Tucson to his patch in the desert, and she was getting hungry. She should have waited until morning to see him, after a good sleep at the hotel.

She had anticipated—even as she buckled her seat belt on the plane in New York—what she would say if Rex asked her to stay the night. She realized that saying no would only lead him to ask, "Why did you come, Dominique?" Why had she? By the time she arrived in Tucson all her thoughts on the subject had canceled themselves out.

"I could fix us something," he said. "Some eggs, if you like."

"What a good idea," she said. Then added, *"Quelle bonne idée."* Introducing French into the room might also conjure up a fluorescent green light from across the ocean.

Rex had set the table and lit two candles. They sat facing each other, eating peppery omelets and drinking California white wine in the light of the flickering candles.

They were both in America now, for the first time in more than twenty years. There was a strangeness in that, as if they were on unfamiliar and not native grounds. She was giddy from the wine and the travel. She felt playful.

"Tell me, Rex, why do you say 'fix us something' and not just 'make us something'? Isn't that cowboy talk? 'I'll fix us some grub.'"

"I don't think so, Red," he said. "But I wouldn't worry about it too much. At least not tonight."

"Certainly not tonight," she said.

"The desert and the sea mirror each other," he said, taking a new trail. "That's what Auden says, anyway. He's right. You'll never miss the ocean, if you stay, Dominique."

"Years ago I would have laughed at your presumption, but I would also have stayed, as I did in Paris, remember? But I'm not laughing now."

"It doesn't matter, darling. This is the time for us to bring it together."

"I feel it could be true," she said, surrendering to a battle she did not want to fight.

She did feel it, her body no longer as tired. Everything else but the room, table, the burning-down candles, and Rex had rushed away and vanished into the night outside. She was having another spell of calm, her breathing slowing, her shoulders dropping.

Rex, too, was calm, she could sense it from across the table. There was little reason left for him to plead now that she had opened the gate and stood at the door.

"But what it means for us I still don't know, Rex."

"We just have to make it up as we go along. You know that's how it always is with us," he said, as if he had never left her alone in Paris, never had a child with Olga, had never made her wait for him in a café drowning in the rain.

"How it always is with us? You mean how it always is with you, Rex. So what's different this time?" she asked, with a little laugh. "Tell me."

"Come on over here, and let's find out," he said.

"I don't know if I want to, Rex."

The words had just come out of her. She wanted him all their time together and all their time apart, but her desire had met a border within her that she had never before been asked to cross.

"Stay," he said. "At least you can crash here. It's a deal to get back."

"It wouldn't be right."

"I see," he said.

She rose from the table, with her wineglass raised in hand, as if to make an after-dinner toast.

"I still want you, Rex. That part's simple."

He came to her and kissed her hand, his lips faintly brushing her skin. "I love you, Dominique," he said.

"I should be leaving soon," she said. "Pick me up at my hotel tomorrow. We can have breakfast and then you can show me the sights," she continued, hoping to staunch his disappointment at her leaving.

"Well, I'm gone in the morning," he said.

She was taken aback, having assumed he was free for however long she had come to visit.

"Oh!" was all she could say.

Not the whole day, just until noon, he explained. He had to
go to help bail out some migrants arrested for being illegals
but really because they were trying to organize the local
migrant field workers. She realized that since she had arrived
they had not spoken about their present lives, that she had no
idea of what he was doing or on what he was living.

"I thought you gave up that line of work when you left
Mexico," she said.

"There's still much to do, don't you think?"

"Oh, I'm sure," she said, without feeling.

She slowly started for the door, not wanting to leave and
not wanting to stay.

"I guess I have to go," she said.

"Just another few minutes," he said. "There's something to
talk about."

"Is there?" she said, wondering whether he was in fact suffering from some serious illness and had waited until the last
minute to tell her.

"It's about Kenji," he said. "I know how to find him."

She felt dizzy and made her way to a chair.

"Find him? Is he alive?" she asked.

"He's very alive. He's well."

She was stunned, not sure whether to cry for happiness or
rage against Rex. "You mean you've known about this and
waited till just now to tell me?"

"I wrote you the minute I got her letter," he said.

"You could have called. Why didn't you call?" she asked, her
anger rising.

"I phoned the university," he said like a boy wrongly accused. "They wouldn't give me your home number but they said they'd pass along my message should you call in."

Call in? What did he know of her life? That she had retired, that she was living in Montauk, that she was ill again? She lived somewhere in his dream where her marriage, her becoming fifty, her whole new life on a cliff, had never taken place.

"OK, Rex," she said, feeling the uselessness of being angry or arguing with him, but she was at the edge of screaming.

"Don't make me wait another second, please," she said, as calmly as she could.

He took an envelope resting on a stack of books on the night table and slowly drew out a photograph and pages of a letter. She impatiently seized the picture from his hand.

Kenji was shading his eyes when the camera caught him facing the sun. It was not a frown, his expression, but something more somber and melancholy and not caused by the light in his eyes. She was sure of that. He was trim and straight in his school uniform, an austere gray, as was the cap in his hand. She was sure it was Kenji, the older Kenji. Birch trees standing in a tight row, like a white fence, behind him gave the photo its only sense of place.

She did not stop crying until she downed a shot of straight, burning tequila Rex brought her. She looked numbly at the photo she would not let him take from her hand. For all the anger she had felt for him in the past, she had never hated him before.

"I never would have let you wait a minute. I would have walked across America to tell you about Kenji," she said.

"Now, Red, be fair," he said. "I tried."

"Why didn't you tell me when I walked in the door?"

"I wanted to warm up to it and get things settled between us first."

She pushed his hand away from her face.

"I wanted to cap off the night with the wonderful surprise," he added. "But you've been in a rush to leave."

"Where is he?" she asked coolly.

"For now, he's with his mother in Japan," he said.

"Why aren't you there now?" she said. "Why aren't we there?"

He began to explain by reviewing and quoting from the letter in his hand.

No sooner had Tamara returned to Japan after leaving Paris and Kenji behind than she quarreled with her parents. More than a quarrel, a raging fight of recriminations.

For spite, she told them about Kenji. From that moment on they would not leave her in peace. They wanted the boy, even though he was impure, tainted by having a white man for a father. The boy was their blood. The only blood of theirs in a male body, however imperfect. Her father made a deal. If she would help them get the boy, they would let her live as she wished, with her usual income. Her father arranged the whole matter, she said. With his power, there was little problem in organizing Kenji's return—as he put it—to her. With his power, he could organize anybody's return. There were people who could do such things for him, and do even more, should he have wished it. And from the moral point of view, the boy, after all, was hers.

Her parents kept and raised the boy, and as she had no desire to see him, everyone was happy, because her father loved Kenji and was reborn after the boy's arrival.

The problem now was that her father had died, following

her mother's death by a year. His money could not shield him from his grief, she said, not, finally, that she had cared. She herself did not want to take Kenji, although for the few times she spent with him at her father's house for the boy's birthdays, she had found him agreeable and intelligent. Still, he was too reserved for her taste.

In compensation for what she did, although she had done nothing wrong but to give the boy a splendid home instead of the hovel in Paris he offered, she wanted to know whether—and without complications legal or otherwise on his part—Rex would like the boy back.

The letter and its narrative meant little to her, Dominique said—all that was past. There was only one part, other than the news that Kenji was alive, that she cared about.

"Well?" Dominique asked.

"Of course," he said.

She felt herself breathe again and went to the kitchen sink to wash her face with cold water.

"Well, there're couple of things to think about here, Dominique. What with the work I'm doing, I won't have much real time for Kenji. And to be honest, I don't know if I can manage the finances involved in raising him."

"That would be no problem," she said, feeling relieved to eliminate one barrier to the boy's return.

"So," he said finally, "I was thinking that you might take him for a while, until I get straightened out."

She was exhilarated at the prospect of having Kenji live with her. It was more than she had expected, not knowing exactly where all Rex's hesitations and qualifications were leading. But then she realized that she did not know where her illness would lead her, now that there were—at best—

treatments ahead. With all the assurances that they had caught the new cancer at an early stage, how sure could she be of how much time she would have to take care of Kenji? But thinking of Kenji alive made her feel more than ever determined to fight for her life.

"I may not have the time myself, Rex."

"Make time," he said. "Isn't that what you rich have, time?"

She winced. "Is that what you think, Rex? What a small view of the world you still have."

"That was unfair of me," he said. "But not entirely, don't you think?"

"I'll have to speak to Eric," she said.

"Sure, of course," he said. "It won't be forever."

He had left Olga's child and now he was prepared to abandon Kenji. Nothing he had ever done had been so selfish and hateful.

"I think we can work something out," she said. She wanted to leave, and leave on an encouraging note. "The important thing is that we've met again. The rest is just a matter of arrangements."

He kissed her and offered to lead her down the tortuous, dark earth road as far as the lighted highway, where she could drive to her hotel in a flash. It was a good idea and made her feel more reconciled about leaving, feel safer in the night where she was a stranger to navigating the road; and it would give her more time with him, even if it was only to follow his old pickup truck. She could see the truck's outlines in the starlight, and then its lumpish form as it sped away down the steep hill.

His red taillights blinked off as the truck took a turn or spun down a hill, only to blink on again when it ran a flat stretch: They were at sea, his truck a boat with running lights climbing and sliding down the slope of a huge ocean swell.

The lights held steady for a while, then quickly began to recede and fade in the distance—as if the truck had rocketed down the road—until there were no more lights.

She didn't know whether to slow down or to accelerate and finally decided to stay on course, wondering, as she went further, if Rex hadn't taken a turn to a yet smaller road without her realizing it. There was nothing to be frightened about, although she did have a little stab of panic, herself under the great dark sky, lost until daybreak.

She stopped and checked the mirrors, thinking Rex might have momentarily gone off the road and was now following her. The mirrors reflected nothing behind her but a pack of desert wolves waiting for her to fall asleep at the wheel. Night and its imaginings, the fearful child in her emerging with the unfamiliar desert.

She started the car and continued on, speeding and slowing up, until her headlights caught Rex's stationary truck and Rex standing beside it looking up at the sky. He came to her, smiling, walking briskly. She rolled down her window as he peered down to look at her.

"Come on out, Red," he said.

She slid out of the car, reflexively turning off the motor and headlights, so that now they were standing in a black night of stars.

"I thought something had happened to you," she said angrily, "that you had an accident or hit something."

"There's nothing out here to hit, Dominique, just wild pigs and coyotes."

"So where the fuck were you?"

"Waiting for you." He took her in his arms, kissing her so lightly at first that she thought her lips had been brushed by a faint breeze. Then again, harder; and again, this time biting her lip until she felt a shiver go through her. He began unbuttoning her blouse, but she raised her hand to stop him.

"It's been so long," he said. "I can't bear not touching you."

"I need to leave," she said.

He kissed her again, on the forehead, and let her get into her car. "Call me at the hotel tomorrow, as soon as you're free," she said.

He gave her a sweet smile. He looked like Kenji when she kissed him and tucked him into bed.

# CHAPTER 34

S HE WOKE EARLY and read the papers over coffee on her room's terrace. Eric had not phoned or left her any message. Which only made her think of him more and kept her wondering whether she had pushed him too far.

She wandered about the hotel, bought postcards, wrote on several and sent none. She was blasted by heat the moment she stepped out of the lobby, and she retreated to a dark, empty lounge. It was too early to drink. She returned to her room and turned pages of *Vanity Fair* until noon, when the phone did not ring. She called the desk. There were no messages from anyone.

By one she had packed her bags. He would have good reasons for not showing up, he always had. This time he would explain that he had gotten caught up in the immigration mess he was trying to solve, was fighting sheriffs and bondsmen and immigration officers, was buying milk for the children of those arrested, was stuck where there was no phone and was nowhere near a phone or a telegraph or a small fire from which he could send up a smoke signal.

Everything she imagined he would say could be true, but what actually had happened no longer mattered, bringing Kenji into her life mattered. By two, she was in the lobby waiting with her bags for the car that would arrive at three. At four she was in the air.

# CHAPTER 35

ERIC WAS ABOUT the house, making his way through rooms or garden paths, installing a painting or a sculpture he had found for her. Or he was rearranging the library with the help of a large man—another in the retinue of full-time cooks, housekeepers, gardeners—who wheezed like a bear as he climbed the ladder to the topmost shelves.

She could go and live with Rex in his one-room chateau in the desert with its dry garden of cactus and mesquite. She might have done that once gladly. A few times since her return from Arizona months earlier, she thought of picking up and joining him and she called her travel agent to book her flight. The feeling diminished with each day but she still had the tickets in her night table drawer, where she kept her medications.

The sea slowly mounted before her eyes, an ultramarine wall rising toward the sky and heaving toward her. At the same time a pain swelled through her, as the sea rose to the window, blocking out all but an upper slat of light.

Out there on the Montauk beach, people were catching the last rays of summer, frying themselves—against all warnings to the danger—on blankets or sleeping under huge umbrellas, or reading the books of the season.

She went to her computer, opening to her journal of fragments.

Freud said that the individual as well as the world was in conflict between its wish for love and its wish for death. She had written that death, Thanatos, not love, Eros, had won the century's last round. She had come to grandiose conclusions, but there were others closer to home which she could more easily justify.

For her, Eros and Thanatos were not distinct forces but were one. That is what she would write and tell Kenji. Like Cupid in Poussin's painting, who had caused Narcissus to drown and Echo to transmute into stone, Love had been her Death.

But she was not dead yet. Even though she had wished she had been, earlier that morning after chemo and the nausea and weakness that followed.

"Is it worth it?" she asked Rose.

"Sure it is. You'll outlive us all at the rate you're going."

"I'll settle for another five years," she said.

Eric was knocking at the door, entering apologetically and, most unusually, before she had asked him in. She hoped that this did not mean there were more papers he had forgotten to make her sign or that something had gone wrong at the last minute with all the legal and immigration arrangements.

Now he was in the room, his arms at his sides, a clumsy smile on his pale face. She moved toward him, her legs still a little shaky. She looked at him, not sure of what she was searching for in his face, his awkward stance—his body frozen in place and yet ready, as if she had fallen into a heavy sea, to dive in and rescue her.

She wanted to reassure him that life between them was as it had been an hour earlier, and that it would be the same in the hour yet to come, as if to say nothing changes, not even the sea, but she could not.

"Oh! Eric," she said. "Are we all set?"

He smiled again and came toward her, extending his arm for her to take.

She had been dressed for hours, anxiously waiting for him; but now there they were, ready to leave the house together for the second time in one day.

They said little. She held Eric's reassuring hand in the noiseless car, gripped it tightly at the crowded arrivals gate at the airport, and released it only when she saw a flight attendant and an official with a silvery badge conducting a slender young boy toward them. His expression was somber, even as he saw her, even when she bent to kiss him, even when he hugged her and pressed his head against her.

"Kenji," she said.